SELLING OUT

MERCENARY WARFARE BOOK 1

ZEN DIPIETRO

PARALLEL WORLDS PRESS

COPYRIGHT

SELLING OUT (MERCENARY WARFARE BOOK 1, A DRAGONFIRE STATION SERIES)
COPYRIGHT © 2017 BY ZEN DIPIETRO

This is a work of fiction. Names, characters, organizations, events, and incidents are either products of the author's imagination or used fictitiously. Any resemblance to actual events, business establishments, locales, or persons, living or dead, is coincidental.

All rights reserved. No part of this publication may be reproduced, stored in a retrieval system, or transmitted in any form or by any means (electronic, mechanical, photocopying, recording, or otherwise) without express written permission of the publisher. The only exception is brief quotations for the purpose of review.

Please purchase only authorized electronic editions. Distribution of this book via the Internet or via any other means without the permission of the publisher is illegal and punishable by law.

ISBN: 978-1-943931-11-8 (paperback)

Cover Art by Zen DiPietro

Published in the United States of America by Parallel Worlds Press

DRAGONFIRE STATION SERIES AND OTHER WORKS BY ZEN DIPIETRO

Dodging Fate Series
Dodging Fate 1
Dodging Fate 2: Extra Fateful, Uber Dodgy

Dragonfire Station Original Series
Dragonfire Station Book 1: Translucid
Dragonfire Station Book 2: Fragments
Dragonfire Station Book 3: Coalescence

Intersections (Dragonfire Station Short Stories)

Mercenary Warfare Series
Selling Out
Blood Money
Hell to Pay
Calculated Risk
Going for Broke

Chains of Command Series
New Blood

Blood and Bone
Cut to the Bone
Out for Blood

To get updates on new releases and sales, sign up for Zen's newsletter at www.ZenDiPietro.com.

1

Cabot reflected on his financial position as he dusted a hand-carved chessboard at the front of his store. His accounts continued to accumulate, resulting in higher and higher numbers. More than he'd ever had before.

War was good for business.

Not that the PAC was in a war. Technically. Yet. But over the past five months, the Barony Coalition had grown increasingly bold, going from minor transgressions against their treaty with the Planetary Alliance Cooperative to outright incursions on PAC planets. Nothing that amounted to much more than inconvenience and annoyance, but more than enough to foretell political upheaval. Cabot suspected he was watching the opening salvos of a cold war.

Day-to-day life on Dragonfire Station had remained largely the same, in spite of significant internal restructuring within the ranks. Cabot hadn't noticed a shift in buying habits of the station's residents, and his shop remained busy.

It felt like the calm before the storm, and few people even realized it.

The station's chief of security, Arin Triss, entered the shop, interrupting Cabot's grim thoughts. The handsome Atalan had been promoted from legate to chief when Fallon found herself too occupied with internal affairs to see to the daily duties of being security chief. Along with that position, he'd taken over her place as the second in command of the station.

Arin made a fine chief. He was well-liked, and a conscientious officer. But Fallon had earned her place as chief before him, and everyone on Dragonfire still used that title for her. Easygoing Arin didn't mind sharing the title one bit. He continued to work with Fallon to ensure the station's safety, though she now focused the majority of her efforts on the PAC's BlackOps affairs.

Not that Cabot knew about any of that. He was just a trader, after all. There was absolutely no reason for him to know about her life in clandestine operations. Not about her branch of PAC intelligence, known as Blackout, and not about her four-person team, called Avian Unit.

Nope. All that was beyond a simple shopkeep like him.

Cabot finished dusting the final chess piece and tucked the polishing cloth in his pocket.

"Morning, Chief Triss." Cabot gave him a proper bow of respect, as befitted a PAC officer. "Can I show you some Bennite sculpture today? Or I just got in a shipment of click-clack games from Blackthorn Station. They're all the rage there." As he spoke, Cabot crossed to the back of the store, pulled one of the handheld games from the shipping container behind the counter, and met Arin in the middle of the shop. He held the game out invitingly.

"I'm just making my daily rounds. Thought I'd say hello." Arin's tone was dismissive, but his eyes had already snagged on the game. He accepted it and turned it over, causing the game to make a clicking noise.

Rule of Sales Number 1: Most people feel obligated to take an item offered to them.

Rule of Sales Number 2: Once a customer has an item in hand, they subconsciously begin to think of it as theirs.

The game was deceptively simple—a person only needed to tilt it to activate or deactivate magnets inside, causing the pieces to shift. The goal was to get the marble into the slot at the bottom, but success was much more difficult than it looked. The little games had become quite a fad, probably because they were so different from the variety of digital comport games that people had become accustomed to. The physical weight of the game and the clicking noise of the magnets were highly appealing.

"I've almost got it," Arin said as he tilted the game this way and that.

He really didn't, but Cabot wasn't going to point that out. "Yes, you're a natural."

Rule of Sales Number 3: Always compliment the customer's taste, talent, or business acumen.

"How much is it?" Arin asked, his eyes still on the toy.

"Ten cubics, but if you promise to direct people who ask about it my way, let's call it a gift."

Arin smiled. "Word of mouth is priceless, right? But I'm afraid I can't. It might look like improper gifting between officers and tenants. I'll pay the ten cubics, but if anyone asks me about it, I'll tell them where I bought it."

Cabot had known Arin wouldn't accept it as a gift. He'd also known that the idea of passing Cabot's name along would be planted in Arin's mind, all the same.

Cabot didn't need click-clack games or other trinkets. Business was the only game he needed.

He provided an infoboard and Arin transferred the cubics before slipping the game into his weapons belt, right next to his stinger. Cabot found it amusing for a game to be stored alongside a sidearm.

"Everything been okay for you down here?" Arin asked as

he wandered slowly around the store, noting a new painting here or an ornate walking stick there.

"No issues, Chief. So far, the tension hasn't caused any trouble here on the boardwalk."

Cabot's shop was on Deck One, adjacent to the docking bays and alongside other stores and a wide variety of restaurants. A prime location for coming, going, and socializing, the boardwalk made for a great place to people-watch. It served as a major part of the social scene for people who lived on Dragonfire.

"Good to hear. If you notice anything, even if it's just a feeling, let me know, okay?" Arin looked too tense these days. Normally he wore a perpetual smile, but not in the past couple of months. Maybe the click-clack game would ease a little of his stress.

"Count on it. First rumble of anything odd, you'll be the first to know."

"Thanks, Cabot." Arin gave him the small, polite bow of a PAC officer to a non-officer subordinate.

Cabot returned the gesture. Such attention to cultural detail and manners was the cornerstone of running a business so closely associated with the PAC.

After seeing Arin out, Cabot leaned one hip against the doorway of his shop and gazed out onto the concourse. Was it slightly busier than usual on the boardwalk, or was he just scrutinizing too hard?

Young Nixabrin Maringo strode into view, looking mature and no-nonsense. Just months before, she had twirled around the boardwalk at the Solar Festival, wearing a pair of feathery wings. The young teenager had curbed many of her youthful ways when she began an internship with the security department in conjunction with her schooling. She was determined to prove herself to Fallon and Arin, as well as her parents, who were not enthusiastic about their daughter becoming a security officer.

When Nix noticed him, her stern expression morphed into a broad smile and twinkling eyes. Every day, she seemed to grow a little bit more into the beautiful woman that, as an Atalan, she was born to be.

"Hi, Mr. Layne. What's new?"

"Nothing much. Business as usual, for the most part. Except I did get a shipment of these." He pulled a click-clack game from his pocket and held it out to her.

Her no-nonsense posture disappeared and she jittered with the excitement of a young colt. "Ooh, I've seen these on the voicecom, but not in person yet!" She twisted it, rather than giving it the gentle tilt it needed.

"Like this." He briefly placed his hand over hers to demonstrate the slight movement.

"Oh, I see. Tiny adjustments. This is harder than it looks."

"All the best things in life are."

She gave him a shrewd look, showing a hint of true maturity rather than the trying-too-hard variety he'd seen from her of late.

"I met the captain the other day, doing a rotation in ops control," she abruptly announced.

"Oh?"

"I never knew her very well. She always seemed kind of a —" Nix caught herself and changed her wording choice, "—a kill-joy." She squared her shoulders and forged on. "But she seemed different the other day. She smiled and even talked to me, giving me some helpful information on tactical plans. It was weird, but kind of nice, you know?"

"I imagine it was exciting for you to see ops control and talk to the captain."

"Yes. But I was thinking... Maybe the way she was before,

maybe it was because being in charge is hard. Harder than it looks."

Cabot smiled. Aha, there was her point. Yes, Nix was growing up and probably observing a lot more than the people teaching her realized.

"I'd say you're exactly right," he agreed.

She extended the game toward him. "I should get going. I still have a few errands, then I need to grab a quick lunch and finish the second half of the day in school."

He waved away the game. "You keep it. I hear those things are a good stress reliever. You might need it, with your busy new schedule."

A tiny frown formed. "But I should pay for it. This is your business."

"It's advertising. Make sure you show it to your friends and send them down here to get their own."

Her uncertainty disappeared. "Aha, so you're just trying to sell more games." She grinned at him.

"You got me."

"Okay. I'll see you later then." She started to scurry off, then remembered herself and squared her shoulders, striding off purposefully.

Cabot chuckled and shook his head as he watched her march out of view.

He was middle-aged, for a Rescan, but her boundless energy made him feel older. The long brown hair he wore in a neat ponytail had started to show some strands of silver. He vividly remembered being her age, though. So much that it seemed impossible for so many years to have gone by.

He'd had the luxury of growing up in far simpler times.

Cabot had only just returned to the counter of his shop

when the voicecom indicated an incoming message. He didn't always answer such calls, often preferring to listen to a playback so that he could better prepare for a conversation.

But it was Fallon calling, not some business associate. She didn't bother with polite bows or smiles or inquiries about his health. They knew each other well enough to dispense with all that frivolity.

"What can I do for you, Chief?"

"Cabot, could you please meet me in my quarters? I need to discuss something with you."

If she was inviting him to her personal quarters, it must be quite a discussion, indeed. His feeling of dread was only tempered by his tremendous curiosity.

"Of course," he answered smoothly, letting none of his concern show. That was the trick to inspiring trust: always show confidence, always appear to be ready for anything.

He nodded politely before closing the voicecom channel.

Cabot's relationship with Fallon was unlike any he'd experienced. Though they'd never socialized, he'd worked with her under high-stakes and high-stress circumstances, and as far as he was concerned, that was the truest way to know a person. Fallon was cunning, professional, and ruthless when necessary.

Which, of course, he respected immensely.

She was also far more than an average officer with the rank of commander. Officially, she and her team of intelligence personnel had taken up permanent residence on Dragonfire Station because it was one of the most important strategic installations in this sector of space. And because it was only practical to have a backup intelligence division to provide checks and balances.

But unofficially, Fallon and her team did work normal citizens never heard about. The division of intelligence known as Blackout was a mere rumor to most people. During the course of assisting Fallon in her operations, Cabot had revealed some of his own unofficial connections and ability to discreetly operate in gray areas.

He and Fallon now existed in something of a clandestine partnership of their own. She, the officer on the inside of the ugliest, grittiest realities, and he, someone who had connections in places that PAC officers could not go.

It was an entirely off-the-books partnership, which pleased him. However, it was also a high-risk one, which did not. He'd known that, eventually, Fallon would ask something of him he wouldn't want to provide.

Cabot's nose for business never failed him, and his nose told him today was that day.

He sat for a moment, wondering what Fallon wanted. Despite his respect for her, and even a secret fondness, he would approach the meeting as he would any other. Business was business.

When he locked up his store and strode down the corridor, it was with the determination of a soldier marching into war.

2

Cabot eased into Fallon's quarters with a casual air, but he noted every detail that had changed from the last —and only—time he'd been there.

Fallon still shared the two-bedroom suite with one of her teammates, but appearances indicated that teammate was no longer Peregrine. Cabot suspected Fallon and Raptor had begun a domestic living situation. He'd never mention his observation to anyone, but information was always valuable. He hoarded it like the Briveen hoarded Brivinium. Personal facts like that could eventually provide nuance to some scenario, allowing a much greater understanding of events.

It paid to be observant.

Fallon gestured at the living area, allowing Cabot to select his seat. She settled into a padded armchair with a relaxed grace that whispered of restrained lethalness. At least to him, it did. She was charismatic and genuinely good, but she had it in her to do things few people could. Cabot respected that.

"How's business?" She leaned back against the chair.

"Nothing to complain about." He ran an idle thumb along

the seam of his chair. "But did you really invite me here to talk about my work?"

Her eyes sparked with amusement, though the rest of her face remained impassive. "I did, actually. I have a business proposition for you."

Those were, perhaps, his favorite words. But he said only, "Oh?"

"A job, more specifically. I want you to take on a mission for me."

Suddenly the conversation seemed to be more about her work than his.

"I doubt I'm the right person for that sort of thing. I'm a trader, not an operative." It was the closest he'd ever come to saying aloud what she actually did.

Likewise, she refrained from asking him details about the gray areas of his own work. What they did not know about each other wouldn't harm them and would allow them to benefit from their association.

Fallon did not seem perturbed by his lack of enthusiasm. "A trader is exactly what I need."

His nose itched, sensing a potentially bountiful payout. Outwardly, he maintained his doubtful attitude.

Rule of Sales Number 4: Never appear eager.

"What do you propose?" he asked.

"Something you're uniquely qualified to do. I want you to broker a deal between Briv and the PAC government."

He'd been prepared for any number of scenarios, but not this. "I'm no ambassador, and I'm certainly not a diplomat."

"Exactly. You can cut through all of the pomp and ceremony, approaching them on a purely business level. You know how involved Briveen rituals are, and you're impeccably versed in them. Diplomatic endeavors take weeks. Trade negotiations are, of necessity, a more expedient matter. You can get the result we need in far less time."

"If you consider a couple hours' worth of introductory ceremonies expedient." Briveen rituals were not for the faint of heart. They required exacting pronunciation of their words, said at precisely the right time, accompanied by specific gestures and postures. Even eye contact mattered.

Being one of the few non-Briveen traders who knew how to engage in such exchanges had been highly profitable for Cabot.

Fallon continued as if he hadn't spoken. "I believe the Barony Coalition is targeting Briv. The planet's location would be a highly strategic foothold for them. PAC officials believe they're trying to put logistics in place before beginning something major. In the meantime, they're trespassing into Briveen airspace, apparently trying to provoke an engagement."

"Have they had any success in that?" Cabot had heard scattered reports.

"A few half-hearted exchanges of potshots. No fatalities or significant injuries. But you've no doubt heard that already. We haven't kept Barony's actions out of the public eye, though we're not broadcasting how we think this could go. That would provoke panic and economic collapse. But we want the public to be aware of Barony's increasing hostility. It will soften the blow when we announce they're no longer a trade member of the PAC. It should also encourage patriots to refuse to work with them."

"It's tough to break business ties," Cabot mused. "Many won't do so without a powerful reason."

"We're not looking to curtail free trade," Fallon said. "Allies have sovereignty in their own economics, even in regard to business with non-allies, so long as they continue to meet the requirements of PAC membership. We don't want to get in the way of planets' livelihoods, which is exactly why we're handling things the way we are. On the other hand, we do hope they've started to at least think about not dealing with a trade coalition that's griefing a PAC planet. Barony is about a millimeter from pushing too far."

Cabot rubbed the plain metal band he wore on his right hand as he thought about how precarious a situation they were in. "So what is it you want from Briv, and what am I to offer them?"

"Simple. We're offering protection. Barony has been incurring on their space and staging some minor attacks against their ships. The Briveen are angry and nervous. PAC command has deployed scout ships, but so far, what Barony has done doesn't require a military response."

Cabot didn't need her to put the pieces together for him. "So Briv is nervous, and since they are a somewhat xenophobic lot who don't care for leaving home, they don't have enough ships to ward off a concentrated attack from Barony."

"Right. We believe that any day, Barony is going to cross the line that does, by virtue of PAC accords, require PAC command to intervene. Based on that belief, we are prepared to offer that intervention now, rather than later. That means a constant military presence around Briv, along with a contingent on the planet's surface to coordinate efforts between the Briveen and the PAC militaries."

Cabot clasped his hands together and tented his index fingers as he thought it over. "That's a big offer. So what is it you want in return?"

"We want Briv to cancel or postpone all of its existing manufacturing contracts, and provide all current and future goods to the PAC, at market price, until further notice."

In the silence that ensued, Cabot arched an eyebrow. "That's quite an ask."

"It's quite an offer," she countered. "Yes, we're asking a lot, but we're providing more. Briv will suffer no short-term economic losses from making the PAC government their sole customer."

"They'll suffer long-term ones. What happens when the PAC pulls out and their prior customer base has gone to new suppliers?"

Fallon dipped her chin slightly. "That's their disadvantage and the price they'll pay for our help. It may cause some future disturbance in their economy. If so, the PAC is prepared to assist. But the Briveen are the premiere manufacturer of heavy-duty combat ships and their components, and we need what they can provide. We're improving the weapons and propulsion systems of every ship we have in the fleet that's more than three years old. We've even pulled outmoded ships from the stockyards for upgrades."

She let her worry show on her face. "Things are going to get bad, Cabot. There's nothing we can do about that except prepare. Barony is looking to reshape the PAC zone. They want to take charge and make this sector of space into a business, driven only by profit. If they have their way, they'll put this galaxy back where it was five hundred years ago. And I'm not going to lie to you—they're strong. They have money and a formidable fleet. They also control a large portion of the food supply. They're going to starve us, Cabot. They'll starve anyone who doesn't ally themselves with Barony."

"You want to choke them out before they choke out everyone else." Cabot felt numb in the face of the idea of entire solar systems starving. He'd known that PAC was at a tipping point, but he hadn't realized how steep or swift the fall might be.

"We're rallying all the agricultural planets and providing them with free equipment, plants, and seeds. We're starting as many crops on as many planets as we can to shore up the food supply. We've put the synthetic food and vitamin manufacturers into round-the-clock production to create a surplus we can rely on. We're even working on trade negotiations outside the PAC zone, but Barony's doing the same thing."

"And there's no loyalty among mercenaries," Cabot murmured. It wasn't strictly true, as even mercenaries had their networks of friends and colleagues. But it was the mantra and the ideal they liked to advertise.

One by one, the pieces fell together in Cabot's mind, forming the picture Fallon and other members of the PAC leadership must have been looking at for months.

But who was he to have a part in such pivotal negotiations? "I'm still no ambassador. These are huge stakes. You're better off with a diplomat."

"I'm better off with you." Fallon stared at him, unblinking. She was kind of scary that way, though he didn't feel endangered. Just impressed. "You know their ways, and how they think, better than anyone I know. I'm not looking for diplomatic schmoozing and flattery. I'm looking to make a deal, and you know how to broker a deal."

"And if I fail?" he asked.

Her eyes narrowed, and he saw the calculation in her eyes. Deciding how much truth to give him. Truth was a commodity like everything else, and should be held close until given a valuable enough reason to offer it.

In this particular situation, the less truth he warranted, the better his outlook was.

"Even if you fail, PAC command will protect Briv. We can't afford to let Barony have it or destroy it. We need the Briveen's factories, their tech, and their expertise. If we don't have Briv's support, it could mean a longer war with more casualties, or it might mean losing the war and becoming subjects of the Barony empire."

Cabot was not pleased with the amount of truth he had warranted. His expression must have revealed his dismay to her, even though he felt he'd been entirely inscrutable.

Her expression softened with sympathy. "It sucks. I know. This isn't the life I signed up for, either. It all comes down to this: are you too small to be a pivot point in history, or are you the kind of man people will someday tell stories about?"

In case the appeal to his hubris didn't work, she added, "Imagine the status points you'll get for brokering a deal like this. I'd expect that to open some very large doors for you in the business world."

He didn't hide his smile. Fallon would have made a good trader. Instead, she'd wasted her talents on the sort of work that no one ever heard about.

She was a hero. And if there was one thing Cabot knew he was not, it was a hero.

"Why don't you go? You know all the relevant facts and, as I understand it, are as versed in Briveen ritual as I am."

"I'm involved in other tactical plans. Besides, like I said, I'd be viewed as a diplomat and the process would be much more complicated. I need a trader. I need you."

"Can I have some time to think about all this?" he asked.

"Yes. But remember, the longer you wait, the less our advantage. Everything is time dependent."

"I understand." He stood and bowed. Normally, he'd engage in some chitchat, steering the topic to apparently random subjects that might reveal tidbits that related to his business interests. Or listening for clues to the goings-on aboard Dragonfire, or the PAC headquarters at Jamestown, or the entire Planetary Alliance Cooperative. But he already had more information than he wanted, so he took his leave.

She walked him to the door and, as it opened, surprised him by putting her hand on his forearm. "I know this isn't your sort of thing. I've had to do things recently that I never expected to do, either. I know you're the one person who can do this."

He gave her a small nod and walked briskly down the corridor, putting her and the entire bizarre situation behind him. But only for the moment.

"Are you sure you can arrange the transfer of that much grain?" Cabot's new client seemed the nervous sort. He kept fidgeting, his eyes darting to the left of the voicecom to look at something Cabot couldn't see.

He, on the other hand, sat still—relaxed, but politely upright, seated in his quarters in front of the voicecom display. That's what many people in the business didn't understand: trading was more than just prices and products. It was an art of a million different cues, all coming together in perfect harmony to make a sale. Subtle things, such as posture, mattered. Perhaps that was why he appreciated the Briveen and their own unique means of communication.

"Of course," Cabot assured the man. "My contacts transport perishables to Earth every day. The grain will arrive in the correct quantity, on time and in perfect condition. I don't deal with anyone who uses substandard storage procedures. I only work with the best professionals who operate under PAC standards."

The human tried to mask his relief, but the man had no chill. Clearly, the minister of something-or-other did not normally handle this kind of thing. But desperate times had a tendency of shaking up everything that used to be normal. "That's good to hear. Your reputation precedes you—you came highly recommended."

Cabot mentally cracked his knuckles. Time for the upsell.

"I'm flattered." He wasn't. The minister had said nothing but the truth. "I'd be remiss if I didn't mention that you could add a metric ton of cargo for the shipping price you're already paying. Is there anything additional you need?"

The man frowned. "It would be foolish not to maximize the shipping capacity, now that costs are so high. Do you have any suppliers who could furnish the kind of fruit and vegetables that do well in long-term storage? On Earth, our apples and potatoes do well in cold storage, but some variety would be good."

Of course it would. Clearly, certain members of the Earth government knew about current goings-on that might just reshape the entire galaxy, and were looking to fortify themselves.

But Cabot said only, "As luck would have it, I know someone who has a large quantity of tango fruit to move. Would that interest you?"

"If the price was right."

"I'll lean on the guy for the best price, and get back to you within the hour."

"Excellent. I look forward to hearing from you."

Cabot cut the voicecom channel and his display went dark. He opened a channel to Doony Kirk. He'd been doing business with the old guy for many years and was all but certain he could work out a deal for the fruit.

Doony's weathered face appeared on the voicecom in seconds. "Good to hear from you, Cabot. What can I do for you?"

"I've got a potential buyer for that tango fruit. What's your best price?"

Doony frowned and Cabot could practically see the numbers flashing in his head. "I was going to get two thousand cubics from a Barony planet, but they're cancelling a lot of their orders. How eager is your buyer?"

Cabot could get right to the point with Doony. "Pretty eager, I'd say. He has dead space on his transport if he doesn't make a deal."

"Try for the two thousand, then. If he balks, get the best you can get for me, with five percent of it yours."

Few traders would show such trust, but any amount was better than a cargohold full of rotting fruit.

"I'll have an answer for you shortly." Cabot broke the connection.

Savvy people with a hint of the truth were stocking up, just in case.

Though he kept himself on the right side of PAC laws, he was an expert in forays into the gray areas the laws and regulations didn't specifically address. Some traders focused on perishables, while others preferred tech goods. Cabot considered himself a businessperson of all profitable markets, with a specialty in exploiting details and loopholes.

He also had a knack for emerging markets, and, by Prelin, a time of change and emergence drew near. And here he was, long-established on Dragonfire Station, a pivotal location in whatever events unfolded.

Not too shabby for a mere shopkeep.

He relayed the offer of the tango fruit to the beleaguered minister, who didn't bargain half as well as he should have. Cabot started high with an initial offer of twenty-five hundred, and allowed the minister to get a 'deal' of only two thousand.

Amateur.

Cabot switched over to the open marketplace and scanned the list of new acquisition requests. He skipped over commodities like medical supplies. He wasn't a ripper, taking advantage of people just trying to survive. Because of them, people assumed *everyone* from Rescissitan was a sleazy cheat who would sell his own mother for a quick few cubics of profit. When in fact, only a select minority of Rescans had a real nose for business, and there were as many human or Trallian rippers as there were Rescan ones. Every species had that tiny minority of people who'd do anything to get ahead.

Nonetheless, it was Rescans who had a reputation among the other species for being stone-cold cheats with hearts full of nothing but larceny. Since that misconception benefited Cabot more often than not, he did little to disabuse people of this notion. Never mind that if he tried, he wouldn't change their minds anyway.

There was no profit in fighting a hopeless battle.

Profit *should* be his only worry. His whole life was about his business. Yet now, a foreign sense of unease plagued him, like a bug chewing on his bones.

He'd made mistakes in recent months. Mistakes he'd never made before. Fallon and Nix both really *saw* him as a person rather than as a fixture in a store. Normally, people viewed him as nearly an automaton, delivering services and goods, engaging in commerce, just as a Rescan trader should.

When he'd first come to Dragonfire Station, he'd established himself as a bland, ingratiating shopkeep. Friendly, but not a friend. He'd been accepted into that role, and he found it comfortable. He liked his life as it was.

He sank to the couch with a long sigh. He wanted no part of political negotiations. He wanted no part of people relying on him. But how could he say no?

A bottle of Alturian brandy still sat in the cabinet of his kitchenette. He considered having some of it, but decided not to. Brandy would dull his senses, and he wanted all of his faculties intact to mull over his problem.

The door chime sounded, and he took his comport from his belt to check the time. It had to be Nix. No one else would come to his quarters. She liked to stop by on her way home, but Cabot hadn't realized how late it had gotten. He hadn't even reopened his shop after his meeting with Fallon.

This thing was already affecting his life. Better to call Fallon now and tell her no before things got further out of whack. He wasn't the kind of person who made a difference. He was the kind of person who sold things.

First the door, though. Before opening it, he took a deep breath and closed his eyes, pulling himself together. No reason for the child to be upset by his distress.

"Hello, Nix." He gave her his patented benign smile, and she bounced in.

Apparently she'd forgotten her purposeful stride again. He was glad. The girl was a breath of fresh air.

"Hi, Mr. Layne. I brought you something." She reached into the bag slung over her shoulder and pulled out a flat disk and a small fob.

"What is it?" he asked.

"I'll show you." She set the disk on the table, handed him the fob, and walked to the furthest point from it. She pointed to the table. "Tap it."

Dutifully, he tapped the disk, and Nix stepped toward the device. After three steps the fob in his hand vibrated.

"Do you feel it?" she asked, her eyes glowing. "It's a proximity detector!"

"I see that." He was confused as to why she'd bring him such a thing, but didn't want to hurt her feelings. "Very nice."

"I made it! As my science project. I figured if I have to do a science project, why not make it relate to my security internship? I keep trying to impress Arin, but he's kind of tough."

That made Cabot smile. "It's his job to be tough. If he was easy, you wouldn't learn as much."

"I know. But I think I finally impressed him with the proximity detector."

"Indeed." Cabot doubted too many people would be keen to have a teenager dabbling in covert surveillance, but he kept that thought to himself. "What did your teacher say?"

"He said he never wanted to see something like that in his classroom again, and that I got the top mark in the class. So I freaked him out *and* aced the project." She vibrated with pride.

Cabot laughed. "You are something else, Nix. PAC intelligence had better watch out. In a few years, you'll have them on their toes, for sure."

She beamed at him. "I thought you could use the detector

in your store. You know, when you're not there. To make sure no one sneaks in."

"That's very thoughtful." He had a sophisticated system in place already, but he didn't want to deflate her puff of pride. "Thank you."

"You're welcome!" She looked at her comport. "I'd better get home. Mom will want me to set the table. I'll see you tomorrow."

This time, she remembered her proper PAC bow and her purposeful stride to the door.

He returned the bow in equal measure, making her giggle. As an elder, and a tenant of the station, he didn't owe the teenager an equal gesture of respect.

When the door closed behind her, he felt like a tornado had spun through his quarters and back out again. A good tornado, though. Nix's friendship had become dear to him, and seeing her was a bright spot in his every day.

"Oh, no," he sighed. Thinking of Nix and the future she should inherit, he saw danger and uncertainty. He didn't want her coming of age in a time of war, or to ever see war firsthand. Her people had already experienced too much of it already.

He had to play his part, however unlikely that part was, to get the PAC past this Barony situation.

"My life in ruins, all for the love of a beautiful girl." He laughed at the absurdity. She wasn't even his kid. But the little devil had wormed her way into his heart, and he knew he'd never forgive himself if she was one of the casualties the PAC counted.

For the second time, he sat on the couch with a sigh.

"I'm such an idiot."

THOUGH HE ALREADY FELT THE noose of obligation around his

neck, Cabot didn't call Fallon. He wasn't ready to officially commit himself to her plan just yet. First, he had to think through how he would pull off such a task.

Rule of Sales Number 5: Don't leave business to chance. Know your market, and be ready to adapt.

If he were to undertake the negotiations with the Briveen, he would want a partner. Serious negotiations were always better when done with someone else. A partnership allowed a wider range of strategies, as well as providing an opportunity for multi-layered data gathering. Two heads were better than one, as they said.

If he were foolish enough to take this job on in the name of the PAC, there were only two people he'd do it with. The first was Fallon, as he had every confidence in her ability to work both above board and within the shadows. Since she was not an option, that left Arlen Stinth.

He lifted his hand to open a channel to her, but paused. Did he want to involve her? She was irritatingly scrupulous, which rubbed him the wrong way almost as much as it earned his respect. How had she ever made a profit with her distaste for gray areas and unspoken arrangements?

But she was brilliant at reading people, and she had a tremendous nose for business. She had an uncanny knack for finding goldmine opportunities that no one else knew to look for.

It was that eye for detail he needed. If he was going to endeavor to work a deal that was more politics than it was business, he wanted her sharpness on his side. In the privacy of his own quarters, he could acknowledge he also wanted her moral compass.

He opened the channel and waited.

She answered quickly and there she was, a handsome, young Rescan woman with strong features and an inscrutable expression.

He recognized the small bit of background behind her: her ship, the *Stinth*. It wasn't uncommon for a trader to name a ship after herself, but Arlen herself was far from common.

"Hi, Cabot. I'm still on schedule. I expect to make it to Dragonfire in seventeen hours. The trip has been entirely uneventful."

"Glad to hear it," he answered. He noted her assumption that he was checking up on her, and decided to examine that fact later. Was he too concerned about her? Did she find him intrusive? Was his interest in her well-being likely to cause him trouble?

Their friendship was an unlikely one. He, the ruthless older trader, should have belittled and dismissed a young upstart who had far too much regard for rules and regulations for effective business ownership.

But he liked her very much. She was a scrapper in a way that reminded him of himself a couple decades ago. She had a spark, too, and he'd unintentionally become her mentor.

The galaxy was funny like that sometimes.

He gave her his most calculating look, knowing it would put her immediately on her guard. "Do you have another job set up after the one here?"

"Not yet. Working on it. Why?" She gave him her own calculating look, and he had to admit it was darn good.

They were like a pair of prizefighters, circling each other and sizing one another up before someone threw the first punch.

"I have something on the hook. It's big, and I need backup."

"But?" she asked pointedly.

"But I haven't decided whether to reel it in or not."

Her eyes narrowed slightly. "Complications?"

"A couple of big ones. It's high-profile and high-risk. High *personal* risk."

The corners of her mouth turned down. "Sounds like a bad deal."

At this point in his career, when he was comfortable with both his income and his place in life, he was far more risk averse than she was. But his assessment made her warier than she might have otherwise been, and that was good. He wanted her wary.

"It has potential to lead to other big things." If he established himself as an official asset to PAC intelligence, he would likely be pulled into other endeavors. He had acquired goods and services for Fallon in the past, but nothing more. This job would open a new door.

Change was his biggest objection. Not the risk or the difficulty, but his status. He'd worked hard to get where he was: a pillar of the trading community, respected by official and private entities alike. He had a comfortable, problem-free lifestyle.

If he became a representative for the PAC—never mind if it was just for a trade negotiation—he'd be selling out. He'd become a government stiff, and problems would start rolling his way because he'd be expected to help solve them.

He grimaced.

"A bad kind of big things?" Arlen asked, her expression growing even more doubtful.

"Possibly. Or possibly good, but just better than I want to be." He sighed. He was too old for this. He didn't want to sell out. He wanted to live the life he'd earned, comfortably away from any official PAC channels or duties.

"Sounds like you should pass on that deal. You could spend that time doing something that's more of a sure bet."

"You're right," he agreed.

She *was* right. He wasn't the hero type. He was a trader. He'd have to be out of his mind to do what Fallon wanted.

But...

"I think I have to do it, though," he admitted.

A sense of resignation swept over him. Nix had unintentionally convinced him that he needed to do it, and he'd wanted Arlen to talk some sense into him. She had, and it still hadn't worked.

It was official, then. He was out of his mind.

3

Arlen's arguments after her arrival on Dragonfire didn't change his mind.

"Barony won't accept that you're just acting as a mercenary. If they find out you brokered a deal between Briv and the PAC, they'll never see you as a neutral party again. This isn't just a trade. This is politics, and politics are bad for business." Arlen sat across from him, tapping a thumb against her knee.

"I know. And I don't want to do this. But I can't not do it." He couldn't explain to her about Nix and how he wanted her to grow up with a secure future. Or that he wanted the same thing for Arlen's future. He had too much pride to admit to such sentimentality.

So he played the profit card. "Some pretty big doors would open up to me. Imagine the cut I'd get on PAC military trade. I'm already working on a PAC station. Might as well go all in."

Arlen's thumb stopped drumming. She sighed and sank back into the couch cushions, looking up at the ceiling. Then she sat up straight and put her mercenary face on. "All right. Let's make a plan."

"Like I'm going to cut you in," he scoffed.

A small smile tweaked her lips upward. "That's why I'm here. You need me. You know it. I know it."

A reluctant smile stole over his own face. "If I agreed to let you come along...I'd be willing to give you a twenty percent cut of my fee."

"Thirty."

"A third for tagging along on a job you had no part in getting? I'm being generous with twenty percent."

"Except my name will be as black as yours as far as Barony is concerned. I'll never do business with them again."

He smirked at her. "You're too moral to work with them anyway. I'd wager you haven't given them so much as a sack of tango seed since their power grab became apparent."

She had a good poker face, but he knew her; she was struggling not to smile.

"Twenty-five percent. Final offer." He narrowed his eyes at her.

She gave up her struggle and grinned. "You've got yourself a copilot."

Cabot needed supplies and a ship. He didn't own a vessel because it wasn't profitable to do his own cargo runs. He outsourced that kind of thing to colleagues like Arlen. Her ship would be serviceable for the job, but he'd put the matter of transportation in Fallon's lap.

He and Arlen joined her the next morning in the office used by Avian Unit and their colleagues.

Access to Deck Four had always been restricted, but it was even more locked down now. Dragonfire now had an admiral sometimes in residence, liaising between the station and the rest of PAC command at Jamestown. It was a big deal to have an admiral there even part-time, especially when Dragonfire's intelligence division consisted only of Fallon's team of four plus two other members of Blackout. As far as public records went, Admiral Krazinski was the senior officer in charge of PAC intelligence. On the internal, more highly classified side of that department, he also headed up Blackout.

Not that Cabot knew anything about Blackout or its presence on Dragonfire. Nope, that kind of thing was way above Cabot's pay grade, even now, and he continued to be entirely clueless about it.

He also didn't know that Captain Nevitt had begun working with them. Nor did he suspect that Arin was also an asset to Blackout. Information like that was far beyond a simple shopkeep like him.

He liked Fallon's teammates, though. Peregrine was as clever as she was tough, Hawk was as much of a teddy bear as he was a tank, and Raptor... Well, Raptor was charismatic, unmatched in his hacking skill, and hopelessly in love with Fallon.

Yet another thing Cabot knew nothing about. Dragonfire sure had a lot of things going on these days that he remained utterly ignorant of.

Cabot and Arlen submitted to a DNA scan to gain access to the lift that exclusively served Deck Four. Once the doors closed, they each entered a temporary code to match their biosign.

"This is some serious security," Arlen said, giving the interior of the lift a good once-over.

Cabot had been through this procedure only twice before. Fortunately, Fallon rarely had a reason to want to speak to him under such strict conditions.

The woman herself stood in front of the lift when the doors opened, and she escorted them to the meeting room. As they walked through the corridor, Cabot glanced at Arlen to see how she was handling the overbearing sense of procedure.

She appeared calm and self-assured. Good.

Many traders he knew would be nervous under these circumstances. But then, many had reason to fear interrogation and imprisonment.

Arlen did not.

Cabot would hardly have presented PAC intelligence with a criminal as his partner.

Fallon gestured them into a meeting room, then followed. The doors swished closed behind her with an odd sense of finality.

Like it was sealing his doom.

Cabot was surprised to see Captain Nevitt awaiting them. She gave them both a slight bow from the shoulders, which was a compliment from the captain of the station to give to two traders.

Cabot had gotten to know the captain better over the past few months. Almost eight years now he'd been on Dragonfire Station, and Nevitt had been the captain for nearly four of them. Until only recently, she'd held herself away from the crew, staunchly devoted to her job and her ambition. As a result, he barely knew her.

"Good to see you, Cabot. Arlen. I'm pleased you two have agreed to take on this mission. I don't envy the work you have ahead of you. Better you than me." Her posture remained relaxed and regal, but a smirk hinted at humor.

He liked this version of the captain much better, and hoped he'd one day get a chance to know her better.

"We all serve the alliance in our own ways," he answered smoothly, with a touch of amusement. "So I'll get right to the point. We're ready to put this together, but need direction regarding ship and supplies. Plus funds."

"Funds for the mission, or your fee for undertaking the

mission?" Rather than sit at the table, Fallon leaned one hip against it, her arms crossed.

"Both," Arlen answered.

Apparently, she wasn't content to let him do all the talking. He didn't mind, but it was something to note. He'd never partnered with Arlen in this way for a business venture. It might prove interesting.

"Fair enough." Fallon brushed back a lock of hair that had slipped forward. One side of her hair was cropped short, but the other side was chin-length and had a few blue streaks in it. The asymmetric, edgy look suited her. Compared to Arlen, she was skinny and fragile-looking, though he knew her to be as tough as they came. He'd done some research on her genetic and cultural lineage, which was particular to Earth. He'd found that her body type was typical for one of Japanese descent.

Rule of Sales Number 6: Know your customer. A little research goes a long way.

"Let's talk about your fee first." Fallon shifted to half-sit on the table. "Rather than a flat fee for the entirety, you'll split a bounty of fifty thousand cubics upon successful completion of the negotiation, plus a half-percent commission on all trade that results from it."

Cabot wasn't sure what to focus on—the fact that Fallon was deliberately adopting such a casual posture, or the massive windfall she was offering. Both were notable and worth further reflection. But then, keeping him off-balance might be her plan.

Arlen opened her mouth, and Cabot knew she was about to argue. A good trader never takes the first offer. But the offer was already tremendous, and Cabot didn't want to be predictable.

Cabot put his hand on Arlen's arm. "Accepted," he agreed.

Arlen speared him with an intense look, but remained silent.

"And our ship?" he asked.

Fallon looked briefly at Nevitt, and something passed

between them. Cabot would have given teeth to know what it was. But Fallon's attention returned to him and Arlen.

"Although the *Stinth* is a fine cargo vessel, and I've seen first-hand that it can hold its own in battle, it isn't as fast as the *Outlaw*. Since speed is a critical factor, I'm going to loan you my ship. It has standard parts, so you can burn hard from point to point, and I'll have mechanics waiting for you, ready to break records in replacing your burned-out fuel coils and realigning the crystal-matrix converter."

Cabot felt his eyebrows raising. He pulled them back down and fixed his face, hoping the others hadn't noticed. It was just such an unusual offer. Fallon was a phenomenal pilot, and as attached to her ship as a mother was to a child. But she was going to loan her ship to them and arrange constant repair so they could abuse it.

The rental cost of such a ship would be huge.

"And your fee for that?" Arlen asked.

"No fee." Fallon looked straight at Arlen, unblinking. "This mission isn't about money. It's about shortening a war we all know is coming, and saving as many lives as we can."

Cabot sighed inwardly. Grudgingly, he had to admit he'd just been outmaneuvered. By an officer.

It was embarrassing.

Fallon had just shut negotiations down, and she knew it. What's more, Cabot and Arlen both knew they were now in her debt for the loan of her ship. An interstellar starship was a precious possession, and the *Outlaw* was dear to Fallon. Since she wasn't charging for its use, a personal debt was implied. The kind that gave her the right to call in a future favor.

Deeper and deeper, into the abyss. But he wasn't the type to just knuckle under.

"We'll need an expense account. There are supplies we'll need." He said it as if it were entirely normal for the PAC to give a trader such a thing.

"What supplies?" Fallon's bottom lip pulled down a fraction of a millimeter.

Cabot smiled, but only on the inside. Outwardly, he maintained his pleasant, courteous demeanor. "Are you sure you want to know, Chief? Once you know, you can't un-know, and we have an important mission to complete, don't we?" He smiled benignly. To do business with the Briveen, there were things he'd need, and he might have to go to unsavory places to acquire those items.

The lip pulled down further, then Fallon pushed away from the table, standing. "Fine. But the expense account will be capped. The PAC is looking down the barrel of hard times. Now isn't the time for excess."

An ugly truth he didn't like but couldn't deny. He needed the PAC. Without it, life would get very uncivilized, very fast. People like him who possessed valuable things would quickly be relieved of them.

There was a reason he lived within the PAC zone. Life outside of it tended to be fast and brutal.

"Of course," he agreed.

Throughout the meeting, he'd surreptitiously watched the captain. He was unsure about her role in the PAC these days. Being a captain was no small thing by itself, but she had an obvious alliance with Fallon and Avian Unit. Therefore, she likely had a relationship with Blackout. He could only wonder what that might entail.

He was living through a difficult time to be a member of this galaxy, and a dangerous time to know things he shouldn't.

But it was always a good day to be a trader. He always had the ultimate ability to adapt and survive.

Hopefully he'd be able to help his friends do the same.

When Cabot and Arlen undocked the *Outlaw* from Dragonfire, he had a strange sensation. He'd never felt anything like it. He'd expected to feel resigned. Chagrined. Maybe a little disappointed in himself and his until-now spotless record of nonpartisan business.

But here he was, in a ship owned by a member of PAC intelligence, scheduled to broker a deal between the PAC and an allied planet. He was as entrenched in the political and the partisan as he could be. And he felt...well, he wasn't sure what he felt. He didn't feel bad, yet he was fully aware that he should definitely feel less than good.

His failure to accurately anticipate his feelings left him irritated. Foresight and anticipation were his forte. His thing. What he prided himself on.

He hid his aggravation beneath his patented veneer of geniality. It wasn't rational for him to find Arlen's standard procedural announcements and occasional small talk annoying. But when he found himself struggling not to snap at her, he stood.

"If you'll excuse me," he said smoothly, "I'm going to lie down for a little while, so I can be fresh to start making plans."

"Sure, take as long as you need. We're two weeks out, even at this speed. The one thing we have right now is time. But don't we already have a plan?" Arlen looked away from the navigation controls to give him a curious look.

He clamped down on a flare of irritation. His emotional disarray had nothing to do with her. "Going to Dauntless is a where, not a what. But mercenary stations are not as predictable as PAC stations. They change fast."

He would have left off there, but this was an opportunity for her to learn about their business. "I need to do some digging. See who's there now, or who's going to be in its vicinity. Find out who has influence and who doesn't. The entire culture of a place like Dauntless can change in days. We need to know everything before we get there, so we can handle business and get back on our way to Briv."

"Right." Arlen nodded. "Let me know what I can do to help."

Cabot edged out of the bridge, or cockpit, or whatever Fallon called this thing. The space was smallish for two Rescans who had larger frames compared to most species and preferred more personal space. Or maybe it was only his mood that took up too much space at the moment.

From the doorway, he said, "Just keep flying and keep an eye out. The last thing we need is for pirates to decide we're worth trying to acquire."

"Don't worry about it. I always avoid the typical trade route vectors, just to be on the safe side."

The edge of his irritation smoothed. He'd brought her along for a reason. She was a good kid, and a good trader. She spent a great deal of her time on cargo runs, and knew what she was doing. "Call me if anything comes up. Otherwise, I'll check in after I've gotten some rest."

"Sure."

On his way back to his small quarters, Cabot thought of what he hadn't yet told her about what they would do on Dauntless Station. She deserved to know. But knowing wouldn't change anything, and she was better off not having to think about it for the next two weeks.

She'd find out soon enough

Arlen made a perfect traveling companion. They split their waking hours so that one of them always sat at *Outlaw's* helm. The ship could self-navigate, but Cabot felt better knowing that someone always had their eye out. He didn't fancy the idea of explaining to Fallon that he had not only botched his mission, but also damaged her ship. Though he didn't think he had any reason to worry about Fallon ever visiting him in the middle of the night, he was a man who knew the value of being risk averse.

Although the days ticked by pleasantly enough, it felt odd not tending his store each day. He hoped the people on Dragonfire were getting the items they needed. He had a single employee who was fantastic with numbers, but hadn't quite learned the art of salesmanship. Lim was a recent addition to Dragonfire. He was a few years younger than Arlen, and an apparent refugee of a rough situation that had stripped him of his past.

Lim didn't talk about all that, though, and had devoted himself to living in the present. Cabot doubted Lim would remain in his employ for long, but he'd been fascinated by Lim's ability to capture disparate groups of data and sculpt them into a startlingly accurate vision of galactic commerce.

What Lim lacked in sales skills, he more than made up for in market projections. Cabot would miss him when he moved on. In the meantime, at least someone was opening his shop each day.

He let out a long sigh, holding a cup of herbal tea between his hands. The next day, he and Arlen would arrive at Dauntless Station and begin equipping themselves for the negotiations on Briv. His two weeks of quiet and near-solitude were about to come to an abrupt end.

He'd put off telling Arlen his intentions, but the time had come. He finished his tea, cleaned and secured the cup, and left the small mess hall.

He entered the cockpit and took a seat.

"I'm afraid I haven't been entirely forthcoming about the cargo we need to procure for our dealings with the Briveen," he told her.

Arlen half-turned in her seat, looking at him with her

blank, ready-for-business expression. He'd have thought she'd be more relaxed with him by now, but so far, he hadn't seen her lose her wariness with anyone. Before this trip, he hadn't realized she had a chip on her shoulder about something or other, but clearly she did.

"Oh?" was all she said.

"We need a variety of ritual equipment and offerings. I have to find something the Briveen will accept as the gift that opens up business negotiations. Nothing I had in my inventory seemed quite right. Also, they'll provide most of the bells and incense and whatnot, but we each need to have custom cloaks that the merchant caste on Briv wears when conducting negotiations."

"We have to wear their clothes?"

He tilted his head, deciding how best to explain. "Not all of them. Just the cloaks. The Briveen are sticklers for proper caste behavior, as well as their rituals. To do business with them on their planet, we must behave as those of the merchant caste would."

"Why haven't you been teaching me how to do that? I could have spent the past weeks studying."

Here was the sticky bit.

"Because merchants must attend negotiations with a same-sex attendant in tow. We need to hire those attendants on Dauntless, then train them on our way to Briv. I didn't see the point of beginning the lessons until we have everyone on board."

Arlen's posture became more rigid. "You never mentioned we'd bring mercenaries on board."

Having contained the truth up to this point, Cabot now changed tactics and went with a tell-all approach. "I didn't think you'd come along if you knew."

"I wouldn't have. I don't do business with people who don't

abide by PAC law. But now that we're only a day from Dauntless, I have no choice." Her eyes were cold.

Cabot regretted the need for subterfuge, but not his actions. He'd been hired to do a job, and he'd do what he must to complete it.

Arlen was a professional. She'd recognize the necessity of doing things the way he had, once she got over her annoyance.

"Tell me everything I need to know." Her flat tone gave no insight into her current opinion of him.

He appreciated that.

"Omar Freeborn. A longtime associate. He's going to act the part of male attendant, though he doesn't know that yet. He just knows I have a job for him. I sent him a message asking him to find a female associate of his that could handle a highly discreet transaction that requires a lot of in-person contact. He's working on it."

"What's Omar's story?"

Cabot had to think about what details she'd find relevant. He knew a great deal about Omar, having worked with him for decades. Much of that history had no bearing on current events. What was important was that Omar was probably his most trusted friend.

"He's hybrid. Works in the PAC under regulations sometimes. Works outside the PAC in the free market sometimes. He specializes in doing in-person negotiations, so he's often brokering deals for other people and taking a cut of the profit. It's a good business. His overhead his low, and he has no hard ties, so he can go wherever he needs to."

"Is he a ripper?" Her tone hardened on the word.

She could have focused on more practical details, but her interest in Omar's business practices gave Cabot an insight into Arlen. She'd had dealings with rippers—something personal and bad. Whatever happened was the reason she had such a strong moral compass. Damn. He wished he'd realized that about her sooner. At least it had little bearing on their current situation.

"No. He's not a killer or a pirate. He'll lie or cheat when he needs to, but he's not a bad guy." Cabot wished he could tell what Arlen was thinking. Her stony face gave nothing away.

"Fine." She stood and stepped a little too close, looking at him hard in the eyes.

He didn't move a millimeter, returning her look. She was displeased, but they worked a hard business, and he'd been at it a lot longer than she had. A trader half his age would not intimidate him.

Her top lip curled and she leaned even further into his space. "No more surprises."

"No more surprises," he agreed, holding her gaze.

She turned abruptly and stalked off.

He watched her go. As much as he liked and respected her, he had a job to do. He wouldn't let friendship get in the way of that.

BOARDING DAUNTLESS STATION was a frosty affair. Cabot felt torn between respecting Arlen's space and giving her the appropriate warnings about a mercenary station. Her keen eyes took in the sleek surfaces and hard people who openly wore weapons as they strutted through.

Dauntless wasn't the dank and greasy place people thought of when they mentioned mercenary stations. It was as clean and pretty a station Cabot had ever seen. People didn't want to do high-dollar transactions in a shithole, so keeping the place shiny and pleasant-looking meant ensuring profitability.

Plus, mercenary stations weren't plagued with regulations like PAC stations were. No minimum required height for second-floor guardrails or clumsy accessibility platforms. On

Dauntless, you looked out for yourself, because no one else would.

Whatever questions or comments Arlen had, she kept them to herself. She nodded tightly when they arrived at their side-by-side rooms and he cautioned her about going out alone.

"Every now and then, a person will disappear from a merc station, and that's just that." He gave her a pointed look.

She pushed into her room and closed the door.

He sighed, wondering how long she'd be annoyed with him. She still had some things to learn about the business.

He entered his room. He'd selected identical quarters for them that were neither austere nor luxurious. They represented the exact median price of the quarters offered for rent on a nightly basis. This ensured that he didn't come across as either a pauper or a spendthrift. Appearances were important.

Besides, from what Fallon had said, now was not the time to pamper himself with PAC money.

The difficulties that lay ahead for the PAC weighed on him. At forty-five, he was no old man, but of a mature, established age for a Rescan. His concerns lay mainly with the younger people of the alliance. People like Arlen and Nix, as well as billions of children whose sunny futures had suddenly plunged into dangerous uncertainty.

It wasn't supposed to be this way. Civilized societies didn't behave like this. He'd always appreciated that Barony's government was run more like a business than any other government he'd ever seen—even that of Rescissitan. He'd admired the Barony Coalition. Sure, he'd seen hints of ruthlessness here and there, but he'd thought those hints were the unavoidable outliers. Now he knew they'd been glimpses of the truth, and he just hadn't realized it.

His lack of foresight galled him. He prided himself on his nose for business. As a man with no family besides his parents and some extended family on the homeworld, he'd made his work his entire life. He was happy with that. He had a knack for predicting emerging markets years before they happened.

But a major organization within the PAC destroying everything for profit...well, that would have been too much even for Cabot to take seriously.

As he sat alone on the couch of his rented quarters, he knew this was the real reason he'd taken on this mission, whether he'd admitted it to himself before this point or not. It wasn't because the job promised a good profit. It wasn't that negotiating on behalf of the PAC would be excellent for his reputation. It wasn't even that he was pretty sure Fallon knew twenty-three ways to kill him with her pinky. Nor was it even entirely because of his fondness for Nix and his desire to keep her safe.

All those things were true. But if he was being honest with himself—and, as long as he was telling the truth, he avoided that whenever possible—his reason was pride. He'd failed to anticipate this move by Barony, and his failure ate at him. Making a success of this negotiation with Briv was his attempt to make amends for it. To avoid being complicit in their success, he had to negate their success.

He leaned back, letting his head rest on the couch. The band of his ponytail dug into a bone and he impatiently tugged it out, letting his light brown hair hang loose.

His life shouldn't be so complicated. His life was about buying things, selling things, and all the delightful details in making those two things happen. He wasn't supposed to be consequential, and people weren't supposed to rely on him.

Where had it all gone wrong?

CABOT WOKE to the sound of the door chime. He hadn't meant to fall asleep leaning back on the couch. Groaning, he sat up and rubbed the back of his neck, which felt like an oxbeast had sat on it. He checked his comport and estimated he'd only dozed for a half hour.

As he got to his feet, the door chimed again. He didn't hurry. He owed the chime, and the person behind it, nothing. In fact, they owed him for waking him up.

"Who is it?" he asked, his voice rough. Only an idiot opened the door to a stranger on a mercenary station.

"Your past, come back to haunt you."

The voice went through Cabot like a knife. He thought about not opening the door. He had a sudden, unbidden fantasy about decompressing all the station's corridors.

"You have to open the door. Omar sent me."

He continued to think about not opening the door. If there was one person in the galaxy he did not want to see, it was Nagali Freeborn.

Her voice came through again. "Come on. This involves your business, not mine, and you have to talk to me if you want the job done."

He hated her voice. Hated how deep and smoky it was, and how it managed to be smooth like velvet and rough like broken glass at the same time. Hated her peculiar manner of speech, accenting every third syllable in a way that made her words undulate. Hated that he had no choice but to open the doors and look at her face.

As much as he disliked her voice, he detested her face.

He drew in a deep breath, straightened his shoulders, and plastered on his trademark benignly pleasant expression. The surest way to annoy her was to treat her as he would any other person.

Ambivalence would also be the easiest way for him to get through this encounter. He'd been playing the role of ingratiating shopkeep for so long that it was as comfortable as his own skin.

Still, he hesitated before pushing the button to unlock the doors. He felt like a man walking to his doom.

The challenging glint in Nagali's eyes hadn't dimmed over the past eight years. He was further irked to note she looked no older than she had when last they'd met. He'd been hoping that time had been unkind to her.

"Still holding a grudge, I see." She strode in, not caring that he hadn't invited her in, or even stepped back to make room for her. She shouldered her way right in. Just like she always did.

She would enjoy knowing she could still inspire such strong feelings, so Cabot lifted his shoulders in a careless shrug. "You woke me. I was merely trying to shake off the haze."

She eyed him with a small frown. "Well, you do have your hair down, so maybe you were sleeping." The frown smoothed and her full, red lips curled into a little smile. "I always liked how you look with your hair loose. You should wear it like that more often. Makes you look roguish."

"Customers don't like roguish. They like polished and polite."

She made herself at home on the couch. "That's right, you're running a shop now. On a PAC station, right? Blackthorn or something like that?"

She knew exactly where he'd been for the past seven years, but he answered as pleasantly as he would have spoken to a potential customer. "Close. Dragonfire."

"Right. How are things out in that sector of space?" She crossed her ankle over the opposite knee and stretched her arms full-length across the back of the couch. Taking up space to convey comfort. An obvious bid for dominance.

Rather than sit, he went to the kitchenette and mixed himself a drink. Normally, he drank water. In the rare event he needed something stronger, straight brandy did the trick. But he wanted something that took time and precision, so he used the standard items stocked in the room to create a fruity cocktail. Just the sort of thing Nagali hated.

"Things are good. Jamestown is better than new. The repairs brought a good deal of business my way. Not that I needed it. Dragonfire's already a hotbed of commerce. But who minds an increase?" He smiled benignly and used an old-fashioned glass stirrer to mix the cocktail.

"Not I," agreed Nagali. "But then, I could never be tied down to a shop. So pedestrian. How do you bear it?"

Cabot could almost admire how blithely offensive she could be.

He wouldn't give her the satisfaction of showing his annoyance. Instead, he smiled and crossed the room to offer her a glass of the bright pink beverage.

She hated brightly-colored food. A pathological idiosyncrasy. He'd once seen her throw a plate of food on the floor because it had come garnished with bright red pepper, which had not been described on the menu.

She accepted the glass and tasted the cocktail. "Ah. Refreshing. You always did make great drinks."

He most certainly had not. He had never possessed any bartending skill at all. He wondered how long they could go on, each pretending to have forgotten or misremembered things about the other.

He took a sip of his own drink and suppressed a grimace. The sickening sweetness clung to his tastebuds. "So, what brings you by? Have some of your little trinkets you'd like me to put in my shop?"

Nagali could put her hand into any commercial enterprise, and if there was a profit to be made, she'd charm her way to the answers she needed. But her specialty, her personal passion, was cultural artifacts. Religious items, historical items, things with an impressive pedigree of previous owners. She saw these items as treasure, and pursued them with lustful zeal.

"No, not today. As I said, Omar sent me to talk to you about this job of yours." She smiled pleasantly.

Cabot had never seen two siblings who looked less like each other. They were both half Rescan and half Zerellian, but Omar appeared to have gotten all the Rescan genes, and Nagali all the human ones. She had a slight frame compared to his burly one, and while they had a similar tanned coloring, her features were fine while his were rugged. She had long, black hair and brown eyes, while he had sandy hair and blue eyes. Omar was the elder by three years, but she looked a full decade younger than her age.

"Let's talk, then." He maintained his pleasant tone and feigned a sip of his drink.

She set her glass down, indicating that she was ready to talk business. "You need a female attendant. I want the job."

He arched an eyebrow in response. Less was always more with Nagali.

"That's it. You have a job. I want it and I'll do it for free."

His eyebrow remained arched. "Nothing is free."

"Fine, free of charge, then. I want payment in kind. Instruction, along with introductions to people I can work with on Briv."

"So, what you're saying is that you never managed to begin a business relationship with the Briveen, and you want to use me as your in."

"Before you say no, let me—"

He cut her off. "You're hired."

Oh, it was delightful to see the genuine surprise and confusion on her face. Knocking her off-kilter almost made hiring her worth it.

"What?" Her forehead crinkled and all of her slick words had dried up.

Letting his cloak of blandness fall, his tone sharpened. "Don't get me wrong. If this were any other trade deal, you'd still be standing in that corridor waiting for me to open the door. But this thing is bigger than me, and it's bigger than you. What's important is that as long as you're working for me, I'll have you by the throat. You won't cross me, because it would mean you won't get what you need. I can trust your self-interest, and that means you're my safest bet for this job."

"I..." She was still at a loss for words. "Thank you."

"Don't thank me. You'll be cursing me when I make you repeat the contrition ritual for the thousandth time and more, until I'm satisfied." He stood and walked to the doors. "Omar will send you the list of items we haven't yet acquired. The cloaks are of particular importance, and he has the measurements for us both. Of course, you and Omar will need cloaks as well."

The doors swished open and he stood there, wearing a pointed expression.

She got to her feet, looking uncertain. She recognized a dismissal when she received it. At the door, she moved to put her hand on his arm. "Maybe we should—"

He pulled his arm back before she could make contact. "This doesn't change anything. My trusting you to act in your own self-interest doesn't mean I trust *you*. This is business."

He fixed her with a cold look, for the first time revealing his true feelings about her.

"Right." Her features hardened and she stepped into the corridor. "I'll look at the acquisitions list and get back to you tomorrow."

"Good." He touched the door mechanism to close it.

Briefly, he leaned against the door. The silence Nagali left in her wake screamed at him. As always, the woman disrupted his life long after she'd left.

This mission had already been a difficult one. Now it would be pure hell.

Selling Out

"You didn't tell me Nagali was on Dauntless."

When Cabot sat down with Omar the next day in his friend's quarters, he felt less than charitable toward his friend of three decades. He and Omar had worked together frequently during their careers, and he wasn't pleased that Omar had sucker punched him like he had.

Omar, to his credit, looked mildly guilty. "Officially, she isn't. She's laying low at the moment."

Not an unusual thing for Nagali.

"But," Omar continued, "what choice did I have? If I'd told you I wanted you two to meet, would you have seen her?"

"No."

"Exactly. And we need her. I only did what the job required me to do."

Cabot was reminded of Arlen's displeasure at how he had played her. Now he was on the other side of the play, and it was by far the less likeable position. He couldn't disagree with Omar's logic, though. "Fine. But you could have at least warned me that she was on board."

Omar shrugged. He'd do it the same way again, and they both knew it. "She said she had a source for the camphor and the red silk. And a tailor has already started on the cloaks."

"Good. That just leaves me to find something special for the initial offering."

"No hints on what that might be? If I put out a call, I'd know within an hour if it was on Dauntless."

Cabot picked a piece of lint off his pants, displeased with Omar's choice of furniture upholstery. He tried to imagine having such poor taste. Omar made his home here, and while the quarters themselves were fine, his furnishings were an eclectic mishmash of gaudy items, unified only by their expensiveness.

Expensive things had no warranty against ugliness.

"That's the problem," Cabot said. "It needs to be something unusual. Rare. Not necessarily expensive, but something that can't easily be found elsewhere. I need to browse and see what I can find. Surely someone here has something unusual that the Briveen would appreciate."

Omar rubbed his chin, screwing his face up as he thought. "I know a few people that trade in oddities. I'll make some appointments for you."

As a trader, Cabot had access to storerooms and cargo holds that the average customer did not. He could go where outsiders could not, and view items that were not publicly displayed. And Omar could guide him to the right people to see.

"Thank you. That would be helpful." Having Omar make the introductions would speed things up and probably result in a better price. The guy was a big deal in mercenary circles.

Speaking of people who were a big deal… "I haven't had a chance to pay my respects to Overseer Caine. How has she been?"

Ditnya Caine was a legend in the business. Cabot had long admired her. She was a good twenty years older and ran a large consortium from her position as the overseer of Dauntless.

"Same as always. She's not on the station at the moment, though. She's been busy lately."

Not surprising, given all that was happening.

Cabot's comport vibrated, alerting him to an incoming message. He took it from his belt and saw a text-only message from Arlen. She was still miffed, but not so much that she hadn't let him know she intended to leave her quarters in twenty minutes, whether or not he was there.

"Problem?" Omar asked.

"No, not really. Remember that young colleague I told you about?"

"Sure."

Cabot continued, "She's annoyed with me. She'll get over it, but until she does, she might be inclined to go wandering around on her own. She's tough, but young, and not too versed with stations like this because of her personal dislike for rippers and those who associate with them." He brought up a picture of Arlen and passed the comport to Omar. "Can you put the word out that she's not to be messed with?"

Omar took a long look. "Nice. I mean, no problem. But if she doesn't know how things work around here, you'd better keep an eye on her. Just because my associates won't touch her doesn't mean she's safe."

"I know."

Omar let a few beats go by before saying, "So when you say, 'mess with…'"

Cabot made a slashing motion. "Forget it. She's way too good for you."

"But you and she aren't a thing, right?"

"No way. She's every bit as too young for me as I am too old for her."

Omar shrugged. "I'm younger than you."

"Not by that much."

"Still." Omar sent him a questioning look.

"Arlen makes her own decisions. Ask her out if you want. But she'll shoot you down. Guaranteed."

Omar frowned and said defensively, "I can be charming."

"It's not about you. I've never seen her date anyone, or even look appreciatively at someone. She's married to her work, and she has something to prove. Between you and me, I think there's something in her past she hasn't told me."

"There always is."

Cabot smiled. Omar was smarter than people thought. His particular brand was to feign an oblivious sort of ignorance, causing people to let their guard down. He'd gotten so accustomed to doing so that he did it even in private. It was an occupational hazard that Cabot well understood. Every now and then, though, Omar's true self peeped through.

"Right." On his way out, Cabot remembered to add, "But no more surprises when it comes to your sister, got it?"

Omar gave him a grin. "Sure thing."

For Omar, that either meant, "Absolutely!" or "You're an idiot for even asking," and there was no way of telling which.

Arlen didn't smile when she joined him in the corridor outside her room, but she didn't spit in his eye, either. Cabot considered it enough of a win.

"I expect to have some appointments later today, but in the meantime, I'm pretty much at your disposal. What would you like to do? Have you eaten yet?"

She fell into step beside him. "Yes, I ordered room service. I was surprised by how delicious the food was."

He'd expected a simple yes or no, so the additional words were an unexpected bounty. The edge must have worn off her annoyance with him if she wanted to have an actual conversation.

Encouraged, he said, "You can count on excellent service on mercenary stations. Being an entirely free market, bad service gets pushed out almost immediately. If you try to charge someone for a poor service, you'll end up getting a good look at your own insides."

"Nice." Her dry tone belied her rueful smirk.

He shrugged. "It's just business."

"And you're okay with that?"

"Well, I don't work on a mercenary station, do I? There's a difference between accepting the way things are and wanting to be a part of them."

"I know. Of course, I know that." She sighed. "I just haven't quite gotten the hang of mixing business and friends."

"It's a tricky formula sometimes," he agreed. "It was never my intent to upset you."

"I know that too. It's not you I'm angry with. I've just been irritated with myself for being irritated at you. How do you learn not to take it personally when a friend screws you over?"

He wished he had an easy answer for her. "The truth is, it's the hardest thing to learn about business. What you have to ask yourself is whether someone will have your back if a deal goes south, or whether they'd sell you out for an extra percentage of profit. If you find someone who will have your back, then you have to ignore the occasional professional screwing over. That part's just business."

"You wouldn't take it personally if I overcharged you for a shipment or shorted you on an order?"

Cabot clasped his hands behind him as they walked. "No. If I failed to notice such a thing, I'd deserve to pay the price for it. It's the manner and the nature of the cheating that matters. Straightforward cheating like that is so expected that it's practically good manners."

She barked out a laugh at that. "I never thought of it like that."

He continued, "There are some business offenses that will harm a personal relationship. There are lines you can't cross without paying the price. Just like I paid the price of your annoyance for manipulating you. I knew I'd pay, but it was worth it to get what I needed."

"What if your manipulation had meant losing my friendship altogether? Would you have still done it?"

Cabot didn't care for questions that had no answer the asker would want to hear. "Under any other circumstances, no. I would not like to lose your friendship. But this thing we're doing is not just any job. Too much rides on it for me to be precious about whether someone likes me or not. The cost of failure in this endeavor is not one I'm willing to pay."

"Good."

He looked at her in surprise. "Good?"

"If you were the kind of person who would put his own needs above something so serious, you wouldn't be someone I could be friends with."

He smiled. "So, you're glad I screwed you over."

She laughed. "You made the right decision. That doesn't mean I'm going to like how it affects me personally."

"Ah, so we're on the same page."

She shot him a look of amusement. "I guess you could say that. But if these friends of yours are on a different page, I reserve the right to hold it against you."

Given how recently he'd withheld information from her, he decided he had to be forthcoming. "Omar's fine. But Nagali is a different story. If you called her a ripper, I'm not sure even Omar could argue."

Arlen stopped walking. Cabot kept going.

He said, "I know. We need to talk about this, and we will, but not here."

She caught up to him. "As soon as we're somewhere private, I want all the details. Every single one."

"I promise. And those are two words I try very hard never to say."

"Okay, then. Since we're already headed this direction, first you can show me Dauntless. Afterward, you'll tell me everything."

"Agreed." He decided to make it an extra-long tour.

DAUNTLESS HAD TWO FUNCTIONS. The first was to serve as a place where customers could connect with traders and mercenaries. The second was to provide a place outside of the PAC zone where traders and mercenaries could work with one another. A business-to-business venue, so to speak.

Cabot first showed Arlen the public side of Dauntless.

He'd always thought the station to be one of the better examples of its kind. Being at the fringe of PAC space gave it a mix of upstanding and shady people, which naturally created some intrigue here and there. As a result, Dauntless had a charged, electrical sort of atmosphere. Cabot found it invigorating.

Judging by the sparkle in Arlen's eyes, she did too. It was fun to see her trader blood show itself. Too often, she shoved it under a blanket of propriety.

On the station's boardwalk, a variety of aromas assailed his senses. Everything from Bennite stew to hand-dried leather, occasionally punctuated with the scent of Sarkavian pastries or the sour sweat of someone whose ship had sub-par sanitation facilities. With the shouts of greeting, growls of bargaining, and a generous helping of suspicious side-eye, it made for a heady brew.

Only then, while taking it all in, did Cabot realize how much he'd missed all this. When he'd gone into business on Dragonfire, he thought he'd left all this behind. Some things never made their way out of one's blood.

Cabot remained vigilant, watching for something he could present to the Briveen. Unique things could pop up anywhere. Transient traders set up shop in a designated area of the boardwalk known as the bazaar. Here, one could pick through an eclectic variety of goods, from food to technology to collectibles. The only thing the offerings had in common was that they were items their owners wanted to sell quickly. Perhaps it was a load of perishables nearing the end of its usefulness, or someone needed to make a quick sale to afford fuel or ship repairs.

Frequently, the items on offer had a dubious succession of ownership. There was no telling what one would find, and that made it fun. Most of the time, when shopping the bazaar, Cabot found nothing he wanted. The rare occasions when he found a treasure always kept him coming back, looking to replicate that thrill of success.

He wasn't alone in that, either. He saw the cloaked signs of avarice in the other people browsing the wares. It only heightened the excitement to know that, at any moment, someone else might discover the treasure you were looking for.

Cabot loved it.

He kept Arlen in his sight line as they shopped, though he was subtle about it. He looked at antique books as she ran her fingers over Altrevian silk. While she poked through a crate of assorted mechanical parts, he chatted with the man sitting at the next booth. Cabot made it his business to stay on top of any recent news that might affect trade, so he got through an entire conversation about Dinebian thorn-beetles with the pleasant air of someone who cared. As a party planet with no natural resources, Dineb imported absolutely everything. In order to do so, they had massive contracts with governments and they didn't do business with a single proprietor like him. Therefore, he cared absolutely nothing about Dineb's problems.

When Arlen stood frowning down at the box for a few beats too many, Cabot sidled near. Her unimpressed expression didn't fool him. She'd found something that interested her.

"Anything I should look at over here?" he asked her, purely for the benefit of the little man standing nearby, pretending not to be listening eagerly.

"Nah. Nothing for you. I'm wondering if that catalytic injector would be good for fiddling with. You know how I like to try to resurrect useless parts on long trips."

As much as Arlen loved her ship, Cabot doubted she had the mechanical skills to refurbish something like the rusted hunk of metal she was looking at. But she was smart to pretend to know more about it than she did. The increasingly eager little man probably knew even less.

Cabot loved the opportunity to play bad cop. "That thing? Waste of time. Let's look for something you'd have a hope of restoring to working order."

The man hurried forward before they could leave. "Are you interested in the injector?" he asked, as if he hadn't heard everything they'd said. "It's PAC grade. A high-quality part."

"Maybe fifty years ago." Arlen smirked. "Looks like someone needed to get somewhere fast." She turned it over and it made a dull, rock-like sound against the other items in the crate.

She pointed. "See that edge right there? That's part of the shaft it fused to. Some mechanic laser-torched the entire assembly out of the ship. Then someone else cut the components apart to make them look like they were just old. But that little edge gives it away."

The man bent close, looking. "I barely see anything."

"Exactly." Arlen nodded. She spoke to Cabot. "You're right. I need to stop trying to repair these lost causes. I've wasted too much time that way."

Cabot chuckled and put an arm around her shoulders. "That's my daughter. The patron saint of busted mechanics." He gave the man a rueful smile. "Thanks for your time."

"Wait!" the man said as they walked away. "I'll let you take it for twenty cubics. At least it's something to do on those weeks spent out in space, right?"

Arlen paused a moment too long before refusing. "No thanks."

"Before you go, could you show me the ridge thing, so I don't buy something like this again?" The man picked the injector up and held it toward her, keeping her from moving on.

Cabot hid his smile. He knew where this was going.

The man handed the part to her. Clearly, he knew about Cabot's Rule of Sales Number 2.

Arlen held the heavy hunk of metal at an angle. "See right there? It's tiny, so you have to know what to look for."

"I see, thank you." But when she extended the item for him to take, he kept his hands at his sides. "Fifteen cubics," he offered.

Arlen sighed. She looked down at it, turning it in one way, then the other. "I guess it would give me a chance to try out my pneumatic wrench. I could practice on this so I don't damage a valuable component."

"Excellent idea. You're a go-getter, I can tell." The man gave her an approving look.

"I'll give you five. No more."

"Since I like your industriousness, and appreciate the tip on identifying a damaged injector, five it is." He whipped an infoboard out of nowhere and presented it to her.

Arlen shifted the component to lay across her right forearm so she could transfer the cubics to him. When the deal was complete, she shrugged a bag off her shoulder and carefully set the heavy injector inside.

"Nicely done," Cabot murmured when they got out of earshot. "How much can you get for it?"

She let out a low laugh. "Five hundred. It will take a lot of work, though. I wasn't lying about it being fused. I'm going to have to give it a very long chemical bath and dismantle it slowly as I give it more chemical baths. It'll take three months at least."

"That's a long time. Is the return worth it?"

"Yep. Most of it is just waiting. I'm willing to be patient and put the time in to get it done. That's how I make most of my profit. It's a niche that few people want any part of."

"I'm impressed. I didn't realize you had such a knowledge of mechanical parts." Now that he thought about it, he recognized a trend in Arlen's business—picking up items that others deemed not worth the time. Funny how he hadn't noticed that before. She was industrious and observant.

"Good. A trader needs her secrets." She grinned at him.

He laughed. She was good for him. She made him think about things in a way he normally wouldn't. He admired her energy and ambition. Truth be told, he'd left all that behind years ago. He'd already earned a level of success he could maintain while still enjoying his life.

"What now?" he asked as they reached the end of the bazaar. Having found nothing worth buying, he felt a rising concern about finding a presentation gift for the Briveen. If he didn't dig up something appropriate while on Dauntless, he'd have to get creative. Negotiations on Briv couldn't begin until an appropriate item had been offered and accepted.

"Let's check out the shops," she suggested. "Any idea which ones are the best?"

They headed down a corridor, away from the bazaar. Even on a mercenary station, shopkeeps didn't appreciate sharing space with transients. The established shops offered a more professional experience, along with a much higher price tag. Anything taking up valuable space in a store on Dauntless had to be worth the shop owner's investment.

Cabot would be more likely to find something special there, but if he did, he'd pay handsomely for it.

"It's been too long since I was here. Shops on a station like this have a high turnover. The rent cost ensures that only the most profitable of stores last."

She cast him a sly look. "How would your shop fare here, instead of on Dragonfire?"

He raised a supercilious eyebrow. "My shop would do well on any station. Though I'd have to adjust my practices to fit in here."

"What would you change?" she persisted.

"That's the kind of information that doesn't come free." He smiled to soften his refusal to answer.

She laughed.

She probably hadn't expected him to answer, but it never hurt to ask. It showed his esteem for her, though, for him to imply he was concerned she might steal some of his business away.

The truth was, he was less concerned about his trade secrets than he was about showing his soft side—the one he pretended not to have.

After a good turn at true mercenary trading, he'd lucked into something on Dragonfire that people like him rarely find: a home. A community. Dragonfire, and the people on it, mattered to him. He paid attention to the items the people in his community needed, and what would make them happy. He quietly delivered these things with the impression that he did so purely for profit.

Even if he'd gone a little soft in his advancing years, he didn't want people to know that. Not even Arlen.

Especially not Arlen.

He wondered if she suspected. If so, she didn't let on.

"So, what is it you'd like to find here?" he asked.

"What do you mean?"

"These shops aren't for resale value. The shopkeeps know what they have and exactly what it's worth. So it's not about trade goods. It's about you. What I'm wondering is, what would Arlen buy for herself?"

She rarely showed a great deal of who she was underneath her trader persona. It made him wonder again about her past, and why she revealed so little about herself. Did it have anything to do with her knee-jerk hatred of rippers?

She ran a finger over some textured purple crystals. "I don't need much."

"No, but imagine that on the other side of this store, there's some trinket or treasure, something that speaks to you, that you want to own. Not a part for your ship, not a fancy anti-grav cart for moving cargo. Something for *you*." He gave her a calculated look, of approximately forty percent curiosity, thirty percent challenge, and thirty percent skepticism. It was a well-practiced look and rarely failed.

It didn't fail today, either.

An answer flickered behind Arlen's eyes. She hesitated to speak, but he knew, in her head, she had a crystal-clear picture of what she wanted.

"It's stupid," she said.

"I'm certain it isn't," he countered. He stood there, looking at her, smiling encouragingly.

"It is." she sighed. "I had a music box once. You know the kind with an embedded music chip that you couldn't change out? Old-fashioned. Anyway, it played a song. I don't know what the song was. Something human, I think, because I found similar decoration patterns on other music boxes from Earth made about a hundred years ago."

"Did someone special give it to you?"

"Yes. A friend." The depth of sadness in those three words suggested that the person either no longer lived, or was otherwise lost to Arlen.

"What happened to your music box?"

The flicker of pain he saw surprised him. She contained it almost immediately, but the brief rawness of it made him wonder.

"It was stolen. I always hope I'll find it again, or at least one like it." She forced a bright smile. "So far, no luck."

"I see. Sentiment can lend value."

She turned away, looking at a stack of antique infoboards. "Yeah. Sometimes." Her back straightened. "It's nothing, really."

It was, though. She tried to tell herself it didn't matter, but it did.

"It could turn up someday. You never know." Knowing she did not want to talk about it any further, he focused his attention on an ornately engraved *Go* game. "What do you think of this?"

She edged closer for a better look. "It's a reproduction, about ten years old. Excellent quality." She picked up a playing piece and looked closely at both sides. "The pieces aren't original to the board. They're older, and worth more than the board itself. Altogether, it's slightly overpriced."

He agreed on every count. "I'm sure there's room for negotiation. I'd think about buying it if I ever played *Go*."

"Do you know how?"

"Of course. But I can't remember the last time I played a board game." The game of business had much higher stakes and therefore greater rewards.

"I always liked them." She sidled past the rest of the displays, apparently finding nothing worth closer inspection.

"Shall we move on?" He saw nothing he needed here.

The remaining stores were much of the same—quality goods whose values were well-known by their owners. Arlen found no old music boxes, and Cabot found nothing noteworthy.

He didn't expect to find anything when they strolled into the last store, but his eye immediately snagged on an ancient scythe hanging high on the wall, above the display shelves. Judging by its layer of dust, it had been there a long time.

He quickly moved on, scanning the other walls and perusing the display tables and shelves as methodically as he had in all the other stores.

His thoughts remained on that scythe, even as he and Arlen pointed out this item or that to one another. The Rescan woman in the back no doubt watched their every move and heard their every word, even as she polished a silver tray.

When they drew near her, he said a pleasant hello, as trader custom suggested.

"They don't make them like that anymore, do they?" he asked, looking at the silver tray.

The woman smiled. "They sure don't. And there's a good reason: they're terrible upkeep with all the polishing. Between you and me, I'll take inexpensive, modern materials any day."

Cabot chuckled. "You and me both. I'm afraid I just don't have the patience for all that. But for collectors, it's the care and attention needed that's precisely what makes such an item desirable."

The woman made a sound of agreement. "Collectors," she said with an indulgent shake of her head. "Thank goodness for their foolishness, eh?"

They laughed in perfect understanding. Two steps away, Arlen chuckled as she examined some tiny decorative vases.

"Rinna," the woman said, offering her arm in greeting. Although Cabot appreciated the PAC custom of bowing that allowed people to convey a great deal with small gestures, this was a greeting that represented his own culture. A trader-to-trader gesture of understanding that reinforced a respectful suspicion of each other. He grasped her elbow, as she did his.

It felt wonderful after all his time operating within a PAC station.

"Cabot," he answered. Neither offered a last name. The less others knew about you, the better. Neither of them had any reason to believe they were even exchanging their real names.

It was comforting to be with someone who thought the way he did. Arlen was a good trader, but she was a solid PAC citizen too. A little too good, a little too starched.

Too good for Cabot. Deep down, he still had larceny in his soul. That would always be the difference between him and

Arlen. He put it aside now, in his advancing years, because he could afford to, and his lifestyle warranted it. But that didn't mean greed didn't well up inside him sometimes to bare its teeth when an opportunity presented itself.

Rinna gave him a knowing look. "Spending a lot of time in the PAC these days?"

"How did you know?" Had she sensed his pleasure at their greeting? If so, she was good. And if so, he had to keep a tighter lid on his thoughts.

"I can always tell. The posture's a tiny bit straighter, and there's this hint of a smell. PAC-grade stations and outposts smell different, and it clings to the clothes and hair." She gave him that knowing look again. "And with ones like you, there's a sense of being glad to be home."

Scrap, she *was* good. He'd revealed far too much about himself already.

"Don't worry about it," she said, waving dismissively. "It's not something others notice."

Cabot rarely found himself on the defensive, but he felt that way now. "I'll attempt to slouch more." He rounded his shoulders.

She laughed, showing even, well-maintained teeth and what appeared to be genuine good humor.

"That's an unusual item up there. Is it a weapon?" Cabot pointed to the scythe and let the burden of conversation fall on her.

Her gaze flicked to it, then back to Cabot. "Ancient Briveen farming tool, for harvesting grain."

Cabot made a tsk sound. "Amazing. Can't imagine doing all that manually. But why would Briveen harvest grain?"

"To feed the animals they ate. That was before synthmeat changed everything."

"Incredible. They did so much work to grow grain so they could then grow animals. So inefficient." He gazed at the scythe, impressed with the hard work ancient people had to do just so they could eat.

Rinna nodded. "That's why I'm not sad that scythe hasn't sold yet. I'm kind of fond of it, truth be told."

It could be the truth. More likely, she was making the first move in negotiating a price for it since he'd shown an interest.

"It's a fascinating piece. I might know someone who would like it, but if you're so fond of it, I wouldn't want to deprive you." He gave her his trademark benign smile.

"Oh, I'm just a temporary caretaker, before it finds its owner," she answered. "I'm sure we could settle on a price that would satisfy us both."

And there it was. The opening salvo to a negotiation. It was familiar, like a lover, and just as welcome. Cabot felt the bargaining lust rise in him, just as it was surely rising in her.

It was a dance. A fight. A love affair. All rolled into words and prices and non-negotiable terms.

He squinted at the scythe. "It's awfully big. It would take a lot of space in my cargo hold."

"It's long, but its overall per-cubic-unit shipping size is quite reasonable." She whipped an infoboard from her belt, quickly tapped on it, then turned it for Cabot to view. "See?"

"Hm, not bad," he allowed. Then he moved past the foreplay and into the main event. "How much?"

"Since it's a nearly-mint specimen of ancient origin, its price is four thousand cubics."

Rule of Sales Number 7: An item is only worth as much as someone will pay for it.

"Ah, a collector's item, then." Cabot shook his head. "My friend would only use it as a curiosity in his home. A conversation starter."

The right buyer might pay her asking price. That was the funny thing about such an item. It was useless. It provided nothing but the joy of ownership. Therefore, it was both worthless and priceless. The right collector was out there in the universe somewhere. But it may take a long time for that collector to cross paths with this item. Or it may never happen. Cabot and Rinna both knew that.

"Make me an offer, then," Rinna suggested.

Cabot stared at the scythe. Squinted. Sighed. Finally, he said, "My friend may not even want it, and then I'll have saddled myself with a long, awkward item I have no use for."

"So, make an offer." Rinna's lips twitched in a smile that said she knew he wanted it.

He chuckled. Glancing at Arlen, who stood nearby, quietly watching, he shrugged and said, "I guess I could lose five hundred. If he doesn't like it, I might be able to get that much back out of it."

"I should toss you out right now for making such a lowball offer." Instead of looking outraged, though, Rinna grinned at him.

"So make me a counteroffer," Cabot challenged, grinning back. He was having a fantastic time.

"Fifteen hundred."

"Impossible," he declared. "For fifteen hundred, I'd buy other cargo I could more than double my money on back in the PAC zone. You and I both know I'm not making a single cubic if I have to resell this thing." He peered upward at it. "It's covered in dust."

Rinna pursed her lips. She let out a sigh. "I could sacrifice it for a thousand."

"Seven fifty. We both know that no one else is coming in here this month offering to pay that much for it."

She scowled at him. "Fine. Seven fifty. But no delivery service. You carry it out of here yourself."

Then she grinned, clearly pleased with the idea of him walking through Dauntless carrying a huge scythe.

"I'll arrange for someone to pick it up," he countered mildly.

Rinna pouted. "Fine."

She held the infoboard out and he transferred the cubics to her. "A pleasure doing business with you. Anything else of interest to you?"

"Not today. But thank you."

"How about you?" Rinna fixed her gaze on Arlen.

"Afraid not."

Cabot followed Arlen out, and it wasn't until they were well out of earshot that she turned to him.

"Is that what you needed? I assume you didn't buy that thing because you thought it would look nice in your quarters."

He pretended to be offended. "What, you didn't believe my story about my friend who really needs an ancient Briveen farming tool that's taller than he is?"

"Not for a second."

"Ah well. Yes, it's for the job ahead. I'm not sure it's enough, though. I'd like to find something I can present along with it."

She nodded, looking thoughtful. "How will you know when we have what we need?"

In general, Cabot tried to deal out straight truth in tiny morsels. Information was not only too valuable to spread around willy-nilly, but it could also freak people out. This time, he went with unvarnished truth. "I can't be sure. I've never done anything of this magnitude. That's why I want to try to find something additional. To hedge my bets, so to speak."

"I've never been much of a gambler," she admitted.

"That is no surprise to me."

She gave him a long look, trying to decide whether to be offended.

He helped her out with that. "I like that you're careful, and knowing I can trust you."

She smiled and opened her mouth to say something, but then froze with an odd expression. "What's that smell?"

He'd just noticed the aroma wafting over them too. "Teriyaki chicken, Zerellian style. Delicious. Want to go get some? It's lunchtime."

"Already? That explains how hungry I suddenly am."

"That's the chicken. I'm convinced they use industrial fans to blast the scent out as far as possible. One whiff is irresistible and they know it."

She laughed. "Let's go."

Ten minutes later they both sat down with steaming plates of chicken and vegetables coated in a brown sauce that smelled so good Cabot thought his stomach might turn itself inside out in anticipation.

They didn't waste time with conversation, preferring to devote all their efforts on scarfing their lunch. He wasn't sure where this dish originated, or who might have put their own spin on it. Zerellians might have taken it with them when they left Earth, or they could have invented it themselves.

He was sure there was nothing as delicious as that sauce, which was sweet, savory, and tangy all at once.

After scraping his plate clean, he sat back, sighing with satisfaction.

"Prelin's ass, that was good." Arlen wiped her mouth on her napkin.

Cabot generally found swearing unimaginative and boorish, but in this case, he had to agree.

"I'm having that again for dinner," she declared.

"I'm glad you liked it."

Her expression changed and her eyes tracked to the right of his head. Before he even turned to look, he had a gut instinct of who it would be.

Nagali. Maybe she had some subtle smell he subconsciously registered. Or perhaps she was so self-involved that she actually bent the space around her. He rather liked that idea, as much as he disliked her standing just over his shoulder. Yet standing or moving away would only give her the satisfaction of knowing she bothered him.

He stayed seated and said nothing, forcing her to speak first.

"Teriyaki chicken. Some things never change, do they?"

Finally, he turned his head to give her his coldest look. "They sure don't."

She blinked, and the small movement was a victory for him.

"Omar sent me. He arranged two appointments for you." Her gaze wasn't on him, though. She'd fixed in on Arlen. "Who's your little friend?"

Arlen's chin lifted. "Arlen." She said nothing more, simply staring at Nagali with a look that said she'd be more than happy to show Nagali what her intestines looked like.

"I'm Nagali Freeborn. I'll be your liaison today." She laughed, as if this idea both pleased and amused her greatly. "This should be fun."

It was most definitely not going to be fun.

4

Nagali liked nothing more than to agitate. Her shift to being gracious, entertaining, and pleasant didn't fool Cabot. She wanted to irritate him by showing him just how much fun she could be when she chose. She swept down the corridor, leading them to their appointments, chattering on about entertainments that would be going on that evening and tips on doing business on Dauntless.

The sweeter she acted, the more keenly he hated her.

He imagined what she'd look like flying out an airlock, arms and legs slowly pinwheeling in space, but then felt disgusted with himself for letting her get to him.

Cabot didn't let things bother him. He was pleasant and bland, as a rule. That she could provoke such enmity in him was just another reason to hate her. It was so sadly circular.

If only she looked as ugly on the outside as she was on the inside.

He summoned every ounce of self-control to maintain his passive demeanor, knowing that his failure to react to her was the best way to irritate her.

"Why didn't Omar come instead of sending you?" Cabot

had been clear about his feelings about dealing with her, but, as usual, Omar did what he wanted.

"He had some business to take care of. But don't worry. These two people we're going to see work with me more than him anyway. I'm the perfect person to make the introduction." Nagali smiled brightly.

Arlen had fallen silent. She couldn't know what had happened between him and Nagali, but clearly, Arlen had picked up on the tension. No matter how much Nagali flattered her or offered free advice, Arlen's responses remained monosyllabic and toneless.

Her iciness endeared her to him all the more.

"Have you tried the gelato here?" Nagali was downright bubbly as she glided along between him and Arlen. "Best in this galaxy, in my opinion. Chocolate and tango fruit are the most popular flavors, but my favorite is the pistachio."

Arlen looked straight ahead as she walked. "No."

"She doesn't talk much, does she?" Nagali looked to him for confirmation.

"She talks as much as she needs to. Apparently, she doesn't find you worth the effort." As soon as he said it, Cabot regretted it. The jab at her ego didn't convey the neutral tone he wanted to maintain.

Nagali pretended not to notice the insult. "Ah well. Definitely do try the gelato, though. Oh! And the foot massages at Pralitec's salon. Only Pralitec's, though. The others don't measure up. They'll be gone in no time."

"I might have some gelato later," Cabot said evenly. "Probably not a foot massage, though."

"It's more than just a massage, you know," Nagali said.

When Cabot slanted her a dark look, she laughed.

"Not that. I mean it's medically therapeutic. Feet can suffer from bad circulation in artificial gravity environments. Pralitec's therapists are all PAC-certified health practitioners. The salon

Selling Out

is held to the same standards as those that require inspections. You'll get a full foot and peripheral artery diagnostic. Very health conscious, and much cheaper than the same services on a Bennite hospi-ship. Plus, you get the massage, which is *amazing.*"

"Perhaps I'll try it, if I find the time." He had no intention of it, but equivocal agreement was the path to blandness.

"You'll thank me," she chirped.

He suppressed a sigh. Nagali being nice was worse than Nagali being selfish and obnoxious. It only made him wonder when she would stab him in the back.

Nagali gave him a sidelong glance. "I'm not going to cheat you. Or set you up. You already know that you have what I want. Why would I ruin that for myself?"

He met her gaze briefly and simply raised his eyebrows.

She sighed. "I'm not as bad as you think, Cabot."

"Of course you're not."

"I'm not," she insisted.

"So we're agreed." Hah. It was petty, but he loved the rare opportunity to score a point with her.

"Fine. I'll prove it to you." Nagali stopped in front of a door. "And I'll start right now."

ONCE INSIDE THE slightly underlit quarters, Cabot paused to take stock of the oddity of the situation.

Here he stood, with a friend he hadn't expected to have, and an enemy he hadn't intended to see again. Not only that, but the three stood side by side facing a wizened little Trallian that looked more like a dead tree stump than a trader.

Not that Cabot didn't like Trallians. They were a likeable, small-statured species with bark-like skin and huge eyes. Their facial features gave them the sort of adorableness that kittens and babies had. Most people found them charming. Fortunately, on the whole, Trallians were as sweet as they looked. All species have their outliers, though, and Cabot was looking right at one.

This Trallian wore a deep frown that seemed permanently carved into his face. His large eyes narrowed in a suspicious squint. He sat on his knees atop a cushion, glaring at Nagali.

"Omar said one person. Not two."

She stepped near, smiling down at him. "Two potential buyers are always better than one, right?"

"I don't like it when things aren't as stated."

"It will be worth it, if you have something they like." Nagali looked over her shoulder at Cabot.

Taking his cue, he took one step closer. "Yes, we're looking for something special. Something unique. The kind of thing that doesn't sell often, but when it does, it makes your monthly revenues spike."

The Trallian's eyes narrowed even further, turning them into slits. "No names. Transfer from non-PAC account only."

Cabot resisted a glance at Nagali. Clearly, this guy didn't operate above board. "Not a problem."

The Trallian relaxed slightly, crossing his hands over his belly. "What is it you're looking for?"

He knew he had the Trallian's interest then. He could smell it the way a predator could smell blood. "Like I said, something special. Something that would impress a person who wanted to be impressed. But not because of its value—the cost itself is irrelevant. The gift has to be rare."

The Trallian rubbed his fingers over his chin. "Hmm, interesting. Precious gems and metals are out of the question. What we're looking for is something either so old that there are few examples of it that remain, or something that was made to be one of a kind. Like art."

"I was thinking along those same lines," Cabot agreed. "If

possible, I think my preference would be something innately unique. Art or some handmade craft."

"I have a few things that might work." But instead of getting up to retrieve them, he just sat there.

"May we see them?" Nagali asked in her smoothest, smokiest voice. She leaned closer to the Trallian, smiling more with her eyes than she did with her lips.

"Five hundred cubic viewing fee, credited against any purchase." The Trallian's brow scrunched into furrows.

As much as Cabot disliked looking to Nagali for her advice, she knew this guy and he didn't.

She answered his glance with a nod.

"Agreed." He hated the idea of a viewing fee, though. That meant this guy didn't want people poking around just to see what they could see. Probably because he had something to hide, like stolen goods.

Cabot didn't deal in stolen goods. Not anymore.

The Trallian heaved himself to his feet and shuffled away. "I'll be back in a few minutes."

Arlen's lips were pressed into a hard line, and a look at Nagali revealed only a sunny smile. But that told him nothing. Nagali was a chameleon and a champ at acting.

Arlen's dark expression suggested she'd recognized this man as a ripper. It didn't matter. Cabot didn't expect them to become the best of friends.

While he waited for the Trallian to return, Cabot noted the details of the room. A lightweight jacket hung on a peg near the door. Too small for a Rescan and far too large for a Trallian. Yet it wasn't an item for sale. It belonged to someone who stayed in these quarters. Interesting. He noted a carved bone tea set and a box of playing cards, both of which had recently been in use. He tucked these details away, in case they became useful later on.

Rule of Sales Number 8: Sometimes, information is more valuable than anything.

The Trallian returned with an oddly waddling sort of walk. He carried a large box that obscured his head. He set it down next to the chair he had recently vacated, then took his time settling back in.

When his backside fit into the cushion just right, he reached into the box with a gusty sigh and pulled out a red square. He set it on the table in front of him and cleared his throat.

Ah. An old-school trader. Rather than simply allowing the customer to first examine an item, this guy did it the old way. He wanted to put on a performance, extolling the item's virtues before letting Cabot lay a finger on it.

Fine. He knew this guy's type. But rather than continue to stand, he pulled up an upholstered footrest alongside the table and sat on it. Showing he was not a supplicant, but an equal.

The Trallian did not acknowledge this subtext, instead launching into his speech. "This is an exceptional item, and you'll not find another in this sector of the galaxy. It's a dragon-scale trinket box. Not that it's made from any animal, though. Each scale was hand-forged from steel, and articulated to the others, lining the outside of the box. Piece by piece, it was made by a master metalworker, in a tradition that hasn't been taught for three hundred years. So, this is a truly special item. At least five hundred years old, from the Catozian Empire."

The Trallian ran a finger over the lid and carefully opened it to demonstrate, then closed the lid and flourished his hand at it, giving Cabot permission to examine it closer.

"Hmm, Catozian." Cabot passed a hand over the box's lid, feeling the uniform scales. Its maker had made each individual piece both smooth across its surface, yet sharp along the edges. Not enough to cut, but enough to look dangerous. "Exquisitely crafted."

Like the Trallian had, he opened and closed the box. It was beautiful, and it was unique. But it wasn't right.

"What else do you have?" he asked.

The Trallian immediately reached into the box again and pulled out a larger object. This one was shallow but about the length of Cabot's forearm. Its flat black exterior gave no hint of its purpose.

"Here we have something truly special, for a very particular type of collector. It's a Trivenian hand-torturing device. You see, the hand was inserted here—" He turned the box to display its opening on the front. "And then you push this button." He pantomimed the action. "The machine sends out high-resonance vibration, tuned just perfectly to cause exquisite pain without causing damage to the cellular structures."

"Sonic torture." Cabot immediately disliked the thing. Besides, giving the Briveen such a thing would not strike the tone he was hoping for. "Not the right item for this occasion. Do you have anything else?"

Unperturbed, the Trallian nodded. "I saved the best for last."

Cabot sure hoped so.

The man reached into the box, more carefully this time. He used one hand to lift and the other to steady what looked like a tiny suit of armor.

Except it had four legs, and sparkling gems inlaid into the metal. Even from this distance, Cabot was certain, by the quality of the piece, that both the gems and the metal were precious.

"What is that?" he asked, intrigued despite himself.

The Trallian set the thing on the table, then he quivered with glee. "It's a fully articulated, fully functional suit of armor. For a housecat. In the early days of the colonization of Zerellus, the expats of Earth had two goals. Well, three, if you include survival. But once survival became a given, they wanted to set themselves apart from their home planet by developing their own culture. And status symbols became important. In those days, few could afford an item that is so clearly useless in every way. There are only six of these known to be in existence, and I've only seen one other besides this one. It wasn't in nearly the condition this is. Look at it—it's perfect."

Cabot leaned closer and looked at the smooth curves of metal, the perfect lines, the uniform thickness. The way the legs of the armor, mounted upon a small stand, were both delicate yet strong.

It was perfect. Something so strange, so rare, and so exquisite would please the Briveen. He didn't want to appear too interested, though.

He never tired of bargaining. He lived for it. He had no use for mind-altering drugs or drinking to excess. Putting his nose for business to work at haggling was the greatest high he'd ever get.

"It's certainly well made. And unique, which is what I'm looking for. But it's strange. There's no purpose for it except to sit there, looking strange."

"A conversation piece," the Trallian suggested enthusiastically.

"Hm," Cabot said, noncommittally. He looked to Arlen "What do you think?"

She shrugged, looking unimpressed. "I think something functional might be better."

"You might be right," he murmured, leaning forward to examine the cat armor more closely. He glanced to his other side at Nagali. "What's your opinion?"

"I wouldn't want that." She laughed, the sound deep and rich like caramel. "It's gaudy. But maybe your friend likes that kind of thing." She laughed again, dipping her chin and looking at the Trallian through her lashes.

The trader chuckled. "Personally, it's not my style, either, but it certainly is everything your friend described." His attention rested entirely on Nagali.

Grudgingly, Cabot had to respect her ability to charm and distract. When she wanted to, she had a charisma that could rival orellium as a power source.

"What does something like that go for? I bet you paid a fortune." Nagali asked, sliding in next to the Trallian and half-sitting on the arm of his chair so she could lean forward and examine the cat armor more closely.

Cabot didn't mind her interference in the least. He wasn't foolish enough to think that negotiation had anything to do with pride. It was about results, and Nagali could help get them.

"Me, pay a fortune? Never," the Trallian declared. He appeared to have forgotten that Cabot and Arlen were still in the room with him.

"Oh?" Nagali peeped over her shoulder at him. "What did you pay?"

He looked like he would answer, but caught himself. "Ahhh, you almost had me there." Instead of being annoyed, he laughed. "I've always liked your style."

"I should have known I couldn't trick you." She winked at him.

It took a herculean effort for Cabot to resist rolling his eyes. He knew of no other person who could get away with winking during business matters, or this pseudo-flirtatious flattery. It was ridiculous. It was insulting. It was—

"How about I make your friend a special deal?" The man asked.

It was brilliant.

"You'd do that for me?" she gave him a sly smile.

"For you? Of course. I'll sell your friend this priceless work of art for twenty percent above my cost."

Nagali's smile dimmed. "Twenty? What about that time I

took all those ripe darvan fruits off your hands? If I hadn't, you'd have been stuck with an entire ship full of rotten fruit."

He sighed, but smiled as he did. "Fine. Fifteen."

"And you'll show me the manifest so I can verify it's truly fifteen." She arched a brow.

If someone made such a demand in his shop, Cabot would throw them out.

But the Trallian sighed again. "Agreed."

Nagali looked at Cabot, as if his presence were a mere afterthought. "You agree, right?"

There was nothing for him to do but fall back on his time-worn persona of benign pleasantness. "Who am I to argue with two titans at the controls? I'm just along for this ride."

He gave a tiny bow of his head, nothing like a PAC bow, but far more respectful than the usual in trader to trader transactions.

Within three minutes, Nagali completed the deal. She verified the Trallian's cost, approved the fifteen percent markup, and prompted Cabot to transfer the money.

He was now the owner of a set of cat armor. He could almost laugh about it, except this strange little item would ensure that the Briveen would accept him as a representative of the PAC and begin negotiations.

Time for some major business, of an official and critical type that Cabot had never dreamed of.

He hoped he was up to the task.

"Are you sure we shouldn't have hired a guard to escort us?" Arlen asked.

Cabot's shiny new cat armor was carefully swaddled within a large box of protein bars, and carried nonchalantly on his shoulder.

"No," he murmured. "A guard would be just as likely to attack us and try to steal it. Never mind that people around here would notice a hired guard situation, since that means you had something worth stealing. Pretending we have nothing of significant value is the best course of action."

Nagali edged closer to them and said in a low voice, "Besides, I'm prepared to defend us if needed."

A well-dressed man appeared at the end of the corridor, walking toward them, so they fell silent until they arrived at Cabot's quarters.

Once they were inside, Arlen picked the conversation back up. "How are you prepared to defend us?"

Nagali tilted her head, sending Arlen a look of disdain. "Where did you pick this kid up?"

"She's a friend," Cabot said, with a quiet but sharp edge that told Nagali not to insult her. "She runs an excellent business, and she can be trusted. Unlike some people."

Nagali groaned, a sound of frustration and irritation rolled up together. "It's been eight years! When are you going to get over it?"

He carefully set the box on the dining table before turning to face her. "I don't know if I'll ever get over that. When I even try to think about getting over it, I imagine the faces of those rippers you stole from. They couldn't afford the loss, and they were ready to take it out on me. You nearly got me killed."

"But you're right here. I knew you'd be fine."

"Only because I gave them a five-percent discount on all future transactions and convinced them it wasn't a loss, but a lucrative long-term investment."

Nagali laughed. "Is that how you got out of it? That's brilliant."

He wasn't amused.

She sighed and sank dramatically into a side chair. "Fine, do you want the whole truth?"

"Such a thing could never come from your mouth," he observed blandly.

She sighed again. "Believe me or don't, but here's what happened. I was contracted to redirect those supplies to Atalus. For the refugees of the war. Children, mostly. So you see? I knew you'd get yourself out of it, and we helped a lot of people."

"At a significant profit to you, I'm sure."

"So what? Why can't I help people and make a profit at the same time? Is it a good deed only if I go broke doing it?"

Cabot glanced at Arlen, who was watching the exchange with intense interest. Better if he and Nagali had had this conversation in private, but there was no way to do that now. "Because for you, the profit is what matters and the philanthropy is just a detail you use to justify it."

"That's not true," she insisted, her words short and sharp. "And since when are you Mr. Philanthropy? As I recall, you were always perfectly happy doing things that weren't exactly legal."

"Not exactly legal isn't the same as straight-up theft, or failing to honor an agreement. I may operate in the gray areas sometimes, but I live up to my contracts."

"Is it theft if I'm only lifting goods from someone who stole them to begin with?"

Arlen spoke up. "It is if you don't return them to their rightful owner."

He and Nagali looked at her, but she said no more.

"She's right." He stood behind the couch, not wanting to sit down with Nagali. Doing so would seem like a real conversation, like they had a relationship or something.

Nagali closed her eyes for a moment. When she opened them and spoke, her voice had lost its edge. "I'm sorry about what happened. Things didn't go as I'd planned, but I really was sure you'd be fine. I know I put you in a crappy spot, though, and I'm sorry for that. But I'm not as bad as you think I am."

"You could have told me what your plan was. I could have gotten off that planet before they knew what was happening."

She shook her head. "If I'd told you, you'd have refused to go along with it. And the Atalans really did need those supplies. Which were stolen anyway."

"But it was my life you gambled with. You were always too reckless."

"You used to like taking chances," she answered, but her words lacked the heat he'd expected.

"I have more to lose now." He meant his life on Dragonfire, rather than his relationship with her, but he saw the hurt in her eyes.

She stood. "I'll go. It seems I'm not going to change your mind."

She didn't wait for him to answer. She strode out, chin up and back straight. He almost had to admire that.

The silence in his quarters landed in a heap between him and Arlen. This view into his personal life complicated their previously fairly simple relationship.

"Do you think she really did care about the refugees?" she asked.

"There's no telling with her," he admitted. "The trouble with Nagali is that you can't predict what she'll do, or nail down her intentions. But I'm certain she wasn't doing anything out of pure good will."

"Can you believe anything she says?" Arlen sat in the chair Nagali had recently vacated.

He sat opposite her. "Some would say yes. Some would say no. Strictly speaking, I'd say not exactly."

"She did help us with that Trallian," she mused. "Could she be trying to make up for what she did to you?"

"I don't think it can be made up for."

Arlen's forehead wrinkled. "Why not? Traders screw each other over sometimes. It's part of the business. Just like you manipulated me into being here."

Cabot drummed his fingers on his knee. The truth was poised to spill out, like a man whose gut had been sliced open. He might as well tell her now.

"Because she and I weren't just partners. She was my wife."

ARLEN DIDN'T HIDE her displeasure over Cabot's recent revelation. "When we were on our way here, how could you not tell me that your ex-wife lived here?"

"She doesn't live here, per se. She doesn't really live anywhere. Nagali goes where Nagali decides to go. She's never had any roots to anything. When I checked, she hadn't been on the station in months. There was no reason for me to think that she was laying low here."

"Laying low, why? Had she done something?"

"Of course she did. She's always doing something." The details didn't matter to him.

"You never mentioned you'd ever been married." She frowned, looking offended.

"Just like you've never mentioned a word about anyone you've ever dated," he pointed out. "Assuming you even have. Personal confidences are not exactly in our nature, are they?"

She blew out a long, slow breath and ran a hand over her reddish-brown hair. "You're right. So if we're friends—I mean real friends, not just friendly associates—we should talk more. About personal things. Right?"

She looked so young and uncertain that he had to clamp down on a smile. She was, at her heart, so good and honest. She genuinely wanted to be a benevolent person, and a reliable friend.

It was too bad a strong nose for business put her instincts at odds with her wholesomeness. Or maybe it was a shame her wholesomeness hindered good business. He could see it both ways.

But if her ethical nature kept her from being another Nagali Freeborn, then it had to be a good thing.

But did that mean they had to get personal and share confidences?

He wasn't sure. "Should we? I'm no more accustomed to talking about my personal affairs than you are."

She twisted her hands in her lap. "Shouldn't we? How can we be friends if we don't know basic details about one another?"

"I can't deny that's a good point. I guess I'm just in the habit of not sharing information unless it's relevant and necessary. Fine. Let's try it. What do you want to know about me?" He spread his hands in a gesture of offering.

"Well…how long were you and Nagali married? And was it your only marriage, or do you have more ex-wives stashed across this galaxy?"

"Just the one. She was more than enough. We were married ten years, give or take."

She pursed her lips in thought. "So you went to Dragonfire Station right after your breakup? Which happened right after she abandoned you with those goons?"

"Yes."

"Okay." She nodded, apparently satisfied.

"That's it? I expected more. Questions about the first girl I ever liked, my first sale. That sort of thing."

"Oh, that's a good one. My first sale was selling imaginary cookies at imaginary tea parties. What was yours?"

"You had the nose that early, did you? Well that's interesting, and yet not a surprise." The idea pleased him. Maybe she was right about this sharing thing. "My first sale was my neighbor's hat. He lost it, I found it, and I charged him a cubic to sell it back to him."

She burst out laughing. "That's awful! It was his hat!"

"I wasn't always the pillar of propriety that I am now. And I didn't like that neighbor. He was rude to my mother once."

"Pillar of propriety, right." She smirked. "Is your mother a trader too?"

"No. My parents are scholars. They study interspecies relations and sometimes serve as consultants to diplomats."

She could not have looked more surprised if he'd announced they were naked dancers in a Dinebian nightclub. "Wow."

"They're lovely people."

"So that's why you're so good at dealing with all the different species. You must have picked up a lot from them as you grew up," she mused.

"I like to think it's my natural charm."

She laughed.

"Careful," he warned. "If you keep laughing at me when I suggest I have positive qualities, I might get hurt feelings."

"I doubt that. But I'm sorry anyway. I do think you're charming. It was just funny the way you said it."

"Ah." When she didn't toss another question at him, he asked, "So have we done enough sharing to make us sufficiently in one another's confidence?"

"Not quite. But it's a start." She curled her legs up beside her, looking cozy and more satisfied than he'd seen her on this trip. Possibly ever. "This is nice."

It was, actually. "Well, it's not terrible." He gave her one of his benign smiles.

She laughed again. "So now that we have what we need, when do we leave for Briv?"

"First thing in the morning."

"So soon? Will Nagali and her brother be ready by then?"

"They will," he affirmed. "It's the benefit of being their employer. I can, for once, tell Nagali exactly what to do, and in some cases, she will actually have to listen to me."

"Hm. This is going to be an interesting trip, isn't it?"

"Oh, yes," he agreed. "It most certainly is."

5

Omar didn't bother hiding his appreciation for the *Outlaw*. "This is quite a ride, my friend."

Cabot gave him a knowing look as they carried gear into the cargo hold. "Don't even think about it. This is a loaner, and you do not want to get sideways of the owner."

Omar held his hands up in a placating gesture. "Just asking."

"Right." He frowned at the number of bags Omar carried. "That seems like an awful lot of gear for two people."

Omar lifted a shoulder. "We packed some things that might have trade value."

"I warned you about anything illegal by PAC standards. This isn't just any run. It has to be completely legal and upstanding."

"Everything aboveboard," Omar agreed. "Just normal trade goods."

"I'll need to visually inspect everything. Since time is important here, I'm going to do it while we're underway. But if I find anything that shouldn't be here, we're going to have a big problem."

"Wouldn't expect anything less. But there's no problem."

After strapping the cargo down, Cabot turned to face him. "Good. We've had a good relationship for decades, and I'd hate for anything to damage that. I don't have a lot of what I would call friends. A fact that has just recently been pointed out to me."

"Yep. Not too many guys would be cool with you after you divorced their sister." Omar grinned at him. He had a big, easy grin that was as disarming as it was genuine.

Charm ran in the Freeborn family.

"Speaking of your sister." Cabot arched an eyebrow. "Thanks for that."

Omar chuckled. "Can't blame me. No way do I want to be in the middle of you two. But I'm glad you've got things worked out. With three weeks of space ahead of us, things could get pretty unpleasant in such limited confines."

"First, I wouldn't say things are exactly worked out. But I hope she and I have enough of an understanding for this to work. Second, we need to cut those three weeks down to two. We have a deadline."

Rather than be annoyed by that previously unrevealed detail, Omar looked amused. "Well that makes it extra exciting, doesn't it? How are we going to make that happen?"

"The logistics have been worked out by the owner of this boat, and she had the help of some whip-smart engineers to do it. We're carrying our own replacement parts. The rate at which we'll be traveling, and therefore burning out the parts we normally would not want to burn out, has been calculated. As long as we follow that plan, we'll get there on time."

Omar looked impressed. "I should have demanded more money. I didn't realize we were working with such deep pockets."

"Only as deep as they have to be. This isn't one where we

can pad the bill. It's just that the end result here is of critical importance."

Omar rubbed a hand over his jaw. "Can't say I'm used to being critically important."

"It's a relatively new one to me too, but I'm working on getting used to it." Cabot wouldn't give Omar details about Fallon, Blackout, or their link to PAC command. However, he wanted to be sure Omar knew that the people they were serving were not the kind to trifle with.

"I guess you're coming up in the world, aren't you? Maybe I should set up shop on a PAC station."

Cabot turned toward the door. "That would be quite a change of pace for you."

Omar followed him out into the corridor and the door to the cargo bay closed behind them. "I am nothing if not adaptable."

That was true. Cabot only hoped Omar was adaptable enough to get this job done.

RELATIVE SPEED of travel in space could be at odds with the actual experience of a trip. Whether meandering slowly or going so fast it burned up expensive components, space travel involved a lot of waiting.

The *Outlaw* had autopilot, but most of the time either Cabot or Arlen sat at the helm, keeping an eye on things. Occasionally, Omar took a turn. When Cabot gave lessons on Briveen behaviors and rituals, he engaged the autopilot.

Though his three students were intelligent and keen to learn, the exacting nature of the ceremonies proved grueling to master.

"Don't forget to drop your shoulder for the attrition ritual," he reminded Omar for the fourth time. "Every movement must be exact, with nothing added. If you tilt your head at the same time you drop the shoulder, you're signaling sarcasm. And keep your thoughts focused. We don't have the scent glands that the Briveen use for scent communication, but they can smell our pheromones. Never lie to them because they'll know. Now, let's see it again."

"Right." Omar started over. His shoulder drop was too exaggerated, but at least it was there. They had been en route to Briv for four days, and, overall, his students were coming along well. There would be time to fine-tune the movements once the sequence had been memorized.

He led them through the attrition ritual twice more. "Better. Now, I'm going to pop back up to the helm, but I want you three to remain. Take turns, starting with Arlen, performing the ritual for one another. The other two can critique and correct. Everyone takes two turns with attrition, then take two turns doing the introduction ceremony."

Two groans and a mutter answered him, but no one outright complained. Good enough for him.

As he sat in the cockpit, he allowed himself a long sigh. It was difficult sometimes, projecting his customary affability. The mannerisms were so ingrained in him that usually they were instinctive, but when his nerves got raw, he had to work at maintaining his courteous pleasantness.

Being around Nagali made his nerves raw. Her face, her voice, even her sense of humor were like picking at a half-healed burn from a laser torch: satisfying, painful, and irresistible all at once.

So far she'd been nothing but pleasant. She ignored Cabot's wariness and Arlen's barely masked distaste. She smiled, she joked, and in doing so, she wove that spell that only Nagali Freeborn could weave. The spell that could make the sharpest of businesspeople take a tiny misstep. Just enough of one for Nagali to exploit.

She was one of a kind, that woman.

Thank Prelin, he reminded himself as he checked through his messages at the voicecom. *The universe isn't big enough for more than one.*

As soon as the *Outlaw* had gotten underway, he'd carefully inspected every bit of cargo Omar and Nagali had brought aboard. He'd been so sure he'd find something amiss that he'd been slightly let down when he confirmed that all cargo was within PAC regulations.

Nagali's failure to break the rules made him wonder what she was up to.

He detected no ships in their vicinity, and the *Outlaw* continued to burn along according to plan. In three days, they would dock at Blackthorn Station for some scheduled maintenance that would get them on their way again within twelve hours. Hopefully less.

He wondered what it was like to be able to arrange such a thing. Sometimes he wished he knew more about Fallon and Blackout, PAC intelligence, and PAC command in general. Then he came to his senses and remembered that he didn't want to know. Life was simpler and safer if he didn't.

After indulging in a long sigh and a big stretch that started at his lower back and went all the way up through his fingertips, he sat up again and scanned the ISO market listings. He made some of his biggest profits on such transactions, providing something in his inventory to someone who had a specific need for it. Much of the goods in his storage were intended for just this purpose.

Nagali had always admired his ability to anticipate market changes and the increasing value of items. His skill had combined handsomely with her charisma and smooth talking. The woman could fill a whole room with the brightness of her enthusiasm. She could make a bad deal sound like an irresistible opportunity. Plus, she was brilliant with numbers.

They'd made a good team, back in the day.

Until she'd left him on the receiving end of a lot of righteous anger for her misdeeds.

He shook his head and forced her out of his thoughts. He'd traveled this same mental path too many times over the past few days. The nostalgia was no more welcome to him than her presence on his ship. Fallon's ship.

By the time Arlen relieved him, he'd immersed himself into his financials and the marketplace.

"Anything interesting going on?" she asked as she waited for him to vacate the pilot's chair at the helm.

"Luxury purchases continue to represent a decreasing share of the market. Bulk purchases of commodities continue to rise."

She frowned. "People are getting more and more nervous about the state of the PAC. Barony's incursions will destabilize the economy if they continue."

"Yes. It doesn't take long for the price of a staple item to rise so high that the people who produce it can't afford to consume it. If we get to that point, we'll have many planets thrown into chaos."

"Do you think we will? Get to that point, I mean."

He wanted to say no. The PAC had been a stabilizing force for hundreds of years. Until recent events, it had worked diligently at adding more planets to the alliance, which worked for the collective good of all the allies. Sure, the process hadn't been seamless, or fast, but there were reasons for that, and efforts continued to combat those problems.

But the idea of the PAC fracturing felt surreal. The galaxy was supposed to move toward greater civility, to cooperative behavior, for the greater good of all. For Prelin's sake, the word "cooperative" was built right in to the PAC name. For one entity to halt all that progress and force the galaxy backward into divisiveness felt impossible.

But it wasn't. Greed, once it got a foothold, could destroy anything.

"I can only hope things won't go that far." He switched places with her, leaving him standing over her shoulder.

"We haven't gotten to the point of no return." Her voice held a note of cautious optimism, but wasn't quite convincing.

She'd never said as much, but he now realized that she saw war ahead, regardless of the outcome of this mission. His sadness at this epiphany surprised him. If the young couldn't be optimistic, where did that leave the rest of them?

Every time he went to sleep, he worried that each passing day pulled them closer to a tremendous fall. That the PAC had reached its height and, like many great civilizations before it, would come crashing down. He wondered if the ancient Viseeans or Earth's Roman Empire had foreseen their demise.

Eight years ago, he would have found it all largely academic. Perhaps even interesting, since war can be a tremendous business opportunity. But he belonged somewhere now, and that somewhere—Dragonfire—was at great risk if it all went bad. Along with all the people on it.

He took a breath, finding himself in the unfamiliar position of morale booster. "I can't put faith into faceless organizations, but I know some of the people fighting for us. If there's anyone we can believe in, it's Fallon and the rest of her team. You've seen some of what they can do. I've seen even more. And even that's a drop in the bucket compared to the things I know they've accomplished—though I have no proof of it. Barony is, at its heart, a giant corporation. They can't possibly have anyone who can touch people like Hawk, Peregrine, Raptor, and Fallon."

"Or Captain Nevitt." Arlen's lips curved into a smile. "She's become a lot more personable, but she can scare the pants off me just with a look. You know the one." She arched an eyebrow and attempted Hesta Nevitt's regal disdain.

"Oh yes. I know it well."

He wasn't sure if he'd given her any real comfort, but at least he'd provided her with something to think about. Maybe it would be enough. For now, at least.

"I think I'll go eat dinner, then get some rest." He leaned slightly toward and murmured, "I don't know if you've noticed, but teaching Omar anything is positively exhausting."

As he'd hoped, she chuckled. Omar was learning just as well as the other two, but he and Cabot had a long habit of teasing one another. One of Omar's best qualities was his willingness to be the butt of a joke. He was a good guy. Cabot regretted that they hadn't remained closer since he and Nagali split up. It was his own fault, he knew. Deep down, he'd always worried that seeing Omar could lead to Nagali's presence in his life. And even deeper down, he'd worried that if she were a part of his life, he might end up excusing her behavior.

He walked slowly through the *Outlaw,* admiring its sleek surfaces and pleasing aesthetics. Only someone who truly loved a ship made sure it was maintained so meticulously.

In the tiny mess hall, he tossed a pre-made packet of Rescan spiced noodles into the heat-exchange and waited. He carried the hot dish to a table, then peeled back the covering. Steam and the delectable savory aroma of butter and spices assailed him. It was a smell of home. Not exactly like his mother would have made, but darn close.

"Oh."

Nagali's leathery voice would haunt him for the rest of his life. Even one syllable put his nerves on edge.

"I didn't expect to find you here." She sidled in along the wall, keeping as far from him as she could. "I'll just heat up some food and take it back to my quarters."

He should tell her it was fine. That it was silly for them to avoid one another. That she should just sit.

He didn't.

When she slid the container out of the heat-ex, she gave him a small, sad smile. He could tell she wanted to say something, but she held it in. She lifted one shoulder slightly, then left the mess hall.

It didn't make him feel bad. Nope, not a bit. He was far beyond having any sympathy for Nagali. He'd had eight years to practice not caring about her.

He'd be glad when this job was done. He would return to Dragonfire, and she would return to being a distant memory.

"No, Nagali. In the gratitude ritual, you must drop your eyes when you bow." Three hours into another lesson on Briveen etiquette, Cabot was tired.

"But you said it's insulting to not maintain eye contact. That it implies I think they're too weak to be a threat to me."

"Not in the gratitude ritual. By the time you get to it, you've already established that you see the Briveen as a worthy adversary. So to show deference, you look down, making yourself vulnerable."

Nagali repeated the motion, correctly this time.

"Good. Now the entire thing, from the beginning."

They were all doing well at learning. Much better than that pair of human traders he'd once guided through some basic Briveen learning. That had been a frustrating ordeal. But he'd helped Arlen out of a tight spot, and it had upgraded their cordial business relationship to a friendship.

Fortunately, she, Omar, and Nagali were far smarter than those dullards.

That still didn't make this a fun process. As they neared Blackthorn Station, Cabot looked forward to the twelve-hour reprieve. Sure, it would be only twelve hours, but a dozen hours without a single Briveen bow, head tilt, elbow lift, or shoulder drop sounded like paradise.

They'd all agreed that they'd use the time on Blackthorn as a sort of shore leave. As much as Cabot enjoyed Arlen and Omar, the tight confines of space travel could make it hard to stay pleasant. He anticipated no real difficulties, given that their trip would take only two weeks. But a break from one another would only ensure their continued mutual admiration.

Nagali continued to avoid him, casting him sad looks whenever she had to reverse course.

Not his problem. From what she'd said so far, she'd probably remain on Briv when he and the others left, and that was fine with him.

More than fine.

Setting foot on Blackthorn was a breath of fresh air. Technically, it was no fresher than any other recirculated air from a closed system, but the change of pace was welcome.

Blackthorn had several things in common with Dragonfire. They shared a similar shape and layout, with five decks that started at the bottom with the docking bays and moving upward in both number and location. Deck Five housed the crew quarters, and therefore visitors like Cabot didn't have access. He'd remain on Deck One for the entirety of his brief visit.

This station had its differences too. In size, it was almost double that of Dragonfire. As far as PAC space stations went, the people-housing capacity of Blackthorn was second only to Jamestown—the location of headquarters.

Most of the PAC didn't realize that Jamestown had been briefly out of commission a few months ago. After scuttling the station for security reasons, the highest of the high and PAC command had passed off the repair efforts as a scheduled renovation. Many engineers and mechanics had been drafted into the project, with Dragonfire's own Wren Orritz right there at the head of the repair efforts.

All of that ridiculousness had been handled, but the fallout remained in the form of Barony's little potshots. They knew at least some of how tenuous things had become at PAC command, and it had emboldened them.

Without all of that, Cabot wouldn't even be on Blackthorn, must less be headed toward Briv to do his best at being a diplomat. Or maybe it was less about diplomacy and more about brokering a deal that both sides would find beneficial. But when he thought about it that way, it seemed like diplomacy and trading were the same thing.

Maybe they were, in all the ways that mattered.

Like Dragonfire, Blackthorn's docking bays led right out into the boardwalk, where shops, restaurants, and travelers saw to all manner of needs and desires. Well, all legal needs and desires, anyway. PAC stations were havens for citizens, and as such, they were required to abide by many regulations to keep their inhabitants safe.

Cabot strode along the boardwalk with a small bag over his shoulder. He knew exactly where he was going, and he'd contacted Jim Iwo ahead of time to let him know of his arrival.

Just as Cabot's shop was the trade hotspot of Dragonfire Station, Jim Iwo's shop was a center of activity on Blackthorn. Their clienteles varied somewhat, because although Blackthorn was also a trade hub and a way station, it served an additional purpose as a meeting place for diplomacy. Many admirals, ambassadors, and delegates attended endless trade and peace negotiations here.

That explained why, when Cabot stepped into Jim's shop, the goods on display had, on average, a much higher price.

"Cabot! So good to see you!" Jim stepped in and gripped his right arm firmly at the elbow, in the Rescan style. Jim was human, but was almost as much of a fan of different cultures as Cabot.

"And you, my friend. How long has it been?" He gripped Jim's elbow before letting their arms drop to their sides.

"Six months. Since I dropped by Dragonfire on my way back from a vacation on Sarkan."

"Ah, that's right. It seems like longer."

Jim gestured to a table usually used by customers. A stout brown stoneware tea set had been neatly arranged, with steam curling from the end of the teapot. "Have a seat! I made your favorite."

"Alturian Mountain Blue tea. Very kind of you." Cabot sat, and, according to Rescan courtesy, poured his own tea, then Jim's.

Jim's passion was to serve his customers in the manner they'd expect on their homeworld—unless they preferred otherwise. He even had an excellent knowledge of Briveen communication skills. Almost as good as Cabot's.

"It's not hard to keep some in stock. It doesn't go bad." When Jim smiled, he did it with his whole face. His eyes lit while his mouth created happy lines all the way back to his ears.

Jim was as thin as Cabot was sturdy. Cabot had thick hair he wore long and put in a low ponytail, while what little hair Jim had on the back of his head was black. They didn't have looks or backgrounds in common, but they'd always gotten along wonderfully. Jim had a natural warmth and friendliness —a genuine kindness compared to Cabot's slightly removed bland courtesy.

"How have things been here?" Cabot asked, taking a cautious sip of the scalding tea.

Jim thought for a moment, looking upward before saying, "A little unusual. Lots of comings and goings, as always, but meetings are briefer and tenser. Or else they're unusually long and even more tense. There's a feeling on the boardwalk when things are normal, you know? It's like a pulse. But it's been different lately."

Cabot understood perfectly. He was in tune to the feeling on his own boardwalk. "Yes, things are different on Dragonfire too."

"I'll bet they are! Word is, it's become a sort of auxiliary station for PAC intelligence."

Cabot had to skirt that comment carefully. Officially, yes, Dragonfire served as a remote location for PAC intelligence, as a fail-safe. If anyone hinted about Blackout operating from there, though, he'd have to play dumb.

So he said only, "Yes, it caused a little excitement at first to have a little piece of PAC command right on our station, but in truth, we hardly know they're there."

Jim sipped his tea. "I guess it makes sense that a small intelligence department would be pretty quiet."

"Exactly."

"Oh, you know what would be perfect with this tea? Some Sarkavian wafer cookies. I'll be right back." Jim popped up from his seat and returned a moment later with a sleeve of the fragile desserts. He opened it and spread them on the tea tray.

Cabot plucked one and bit it. "You're right. That's perfect. Not too sweet."

Jim nodded and took a cookie of his own. "A customer recommended them, and now I keep them in stock all the time."

Silence fell between them as the doors to the shop opened. A Zerellian man stood in the doorway, looking uncertain, then shrugged and moved on.

Cabot chuckled. "Get a lot of those?"

"Probably a couple each day, on average. People unfamiliar with the station aren't sure which shops they want, so they take a quick peek. It's kind of funny. I doubt they realize what they look like, appearing, doing nothing, then walking away."

"I'm sure they don't."

"If you have anything private to talk about, I can lock up," Jim offered.

"No need. Just a social call."

Jim's face lit with a gentle, good-humored smile. "I feel like it isn't entirely, but okay."

They both chuckled. Jim was an extraordinarily good guy, but he didn't have the nose. He made a good living, but not nearly as good as he could. It didn't matter. Jim was a station-dweller. An ingrained part of the community. Just like Cabot had learned to be, but Jim had done it naturally rather than by accident.

If Cabot was honest with himself, Jim had been his role model when he'd become a shopkeep on Dragonfire. And he could not have asked for a better example to learn from. Not in terms of business practices, but in finding a place to be, and becoming a part of that place.

"I think I'm getting too philosophical in my old age," Cabot admitted, without sharing the thought process that had gotten him to that revelation.

It was funny, but a decade ago, Cabot would have thought Jim Iwo soft. A product of the PAC. While that was accurate, Cabot now saw those qualities as a plus.

"Age is the great equalizer, isn't it?" Jim toasted Cabot with his teacup. "We gain wisdom and memories, and when we get old enough, we realize all those answers we thought we once had were just hubris."

Was that what it was? Cabot had thought that maybe he was losing a little bit of his nose. Because the thing he never admitted to anyone was that there was only so much profit a person needed. Was that him shedding hubris and gaining wisdom?

"I don't feel wise," he confided. "I feel like I'm just trying to hold the pieces together. Keep my life the way it is. You know?"

"Oh yeah. I know."

"Think it's possible?"

Jim rested his cup on the table. "Not at all. Things are going to be what they are. But what we can do is take care of the people that matter to us."

Cabot stared into the blue-black tea. A swirl of its natural oil spun slowly, extending itself in a longer, yet ever-thinning line. "I guess so."

"Life's short," Jim said. "Have a cookie."

Cabot laughed. From anyone else, the advice would be meaningless—an acknowledgement of futility and mortality. But from Jim, it was pragmatic. A person only has so much time. So he should take all the happiness he could get.

The parts of himself that seemed in perpetual disagreement suddenly quieted, allowing a quiet question to rise in his mind.

What would make him happy?

CABOT DIDN'T NEED an existential crisis on top of everything he was dealing with. But as he left Jim Iwo's shop and headed to the starport, he gave himself and his future some thought.

He found himself a seat in the gallery of Deck One and stared out of Blackthorn Station's most famous attribute: its starport. Many a person had spent some time here, pondering the universe or their future or both.

Sitting in his theater-style seat, Cabot reclined and stared out into the abyss of inky space beyond Blackthorn. Five decks of hull had been created from a translucent material to form the massive starport. Looking up, Cabot could see into the deck above and the immensity of space beyond. He always found it a humbling experience. He couldn't help but feel that whatever his problems were, they were drowned out by the realization of how small and insignificant he was.

Rather than being a disturbing thought, it was comforting.

This section of space had nothing to light it, making the planets and stars beyond stand out like beacons.

A shame Dragonfire hadn't been built with a starport like this. Its fiery nebula would have made for some good viewing during a soul-search. But it was a smaller station, and not built to impress or entertain important diplomats.

"Still mad at me?"

That voice. It went through him like a bolt of electricity.

He turned to find Nagali sitting behind him, wearing an uncharacteristic sadness. Whether she actually felt any bit of sadness, he did not know. But she wore it.

He faced forward again, speaking loud enough for her to hear. "There's a big difference between anger and distaste."

She moved around the seats to sit beside him. He did not consider this an improvement.

"Distaste is what makes you look at me with daggers in your eyes? It's only distaste that has you avoiding eye contact whenever we work on the rituals? I'm not buying it."

He stared out into space. "I'm not selling anything."

In his peripheral vision, he saw her looking at him.

"This is where I make an impassioned speech, insisting I've changed, right? And you disdainfully tell me that someone like me never changes."

He said nothing.

She let out a sharp burst of laughter, though it sounded more of bitterness than amusement. "You'd be right. I haven't changed. But what you have wrong about me is that I was never as bad as you thought. I admit, my handling of that situation was subpar. I thought the guy was working alone, and didn't realize he'd have goons to back him up. But by that point, it was too late to change anything."

"So you thought you'd leave me one-on-one with the guy you'd just ripped off? And I should feel better about it all, now that you've told me that? It wasn't the first time you'd put me in a tight spot, either."

"Up until that point, as far as I knew, you liked the fact that I was unpredictable. You used to say you enjoyed my keeping things interesting. And then, all of a sudden, a job went wrong and that was the point you began to detest the thing about me you'd always said you liked? It was hard on me too, you know. It came as a shock, to be so hated by my husband. Who immediately became my ex-husband, without so much as a word."

Her voice had softened in a way he'd seldom heard, causing him to turn his head slightly to look at her.

"You gave me no chance to try to change," she whispered, all artifice stripped away. He'd only seen her so unguarded a few times over their many years together.

"Trying to change would have made you miserable," he murmured. "And it wouldn't have worked. You can't change your very nature just to please someone else."

"I'd have tried."

In that instant, he believed her. "I'm sorry the divorce hurt you. But it was inevitable. Prolonging it would have just hurt us both."

"You're probably right," she agreed. "Still...I always wished I'd had the chance. To try."

"If I'd come back to see you, I'd have given you a chance, and we both would have suffered for it. You were always a force I could not resist."

She smiled sadly. "And now we are almost ten years older, and my feelings haven't changed."

He had no answer for her that would do either of them any good.

"Are you happy in your life?" she asked when he remained silent. "Living under PAC regulations?"

"Very. So much so that I took on this venture in an attempt to preserve that life." Maybe he shouldn't reveal that much to her. Probably shouldn't.

"How did that happen, anyway? I can't put together how something this big would trickle down to you."

"I know people. I was in the right place, with the right skillset. Apparently."

"The success of this mission is important to you. Not just as a job, or a curiosity to witness, but deep down." She looked at him, truly seeing him in a way that few people could.

"Yes," he admitted. "This matters. And the people I'm doing it for matter."

"Well then." She sat straighter. "I'll have to do everything I can to help you get it done."

They looked at each other. It made him feel raw. And real.

She meant what she said. She'd put all of her energy into getting this job done.

He wasn't sure he was prepared for Nagali Freeborn's full force of will.

6

Though Blackthorn's boardwalk never became quiet, Cabot took advantage of a lull in traffic at an odd hour between lunch and dinner. He commandeered a table right there on the boardwalk rather than one within a restaurant so he could people-watch and enjoy the sights and sounds.

Truth be told, he missed his own boardwalk. He missed seeing Arin on his morning rounds, and Fallon on her afternoon ones. Missed seeing the woman who ran the tea shop and the strangers who came into his shop for the first time. In a blank space within him, memories echoed of the murmur of overlapping voices and the gentle hum of antigrav carts.

The sounds at Blackthorn were similar, but not quite the same as home.

He worked his way through a cosmopolitan meal with slow but steady determination. He had noodles from Zerellus, bread from Earth, and stew from Bennaris. Plus a pot of Rescan tea. He loved that about PAC stations—that they took the best things of all the allied planets within the cooperative and shared them. Actually, that was what he loved about the entire

Planetary Alliance Cooperative. All the peoples together, sharing all their best traits to make them strong.

He watched a pair of young lovers flirt and canoodle before disappearing around the concourse. A father tried to feed two young children. Every time he got a spoon of food into the mouth of one, the other one tried to toddle off.

Cabot liked watching the people who came through the docking bays, luggage in hand, or slung over their shoulders. He could tell by the way they looked around which of them were visiting Blackthorn for the first time and who had been there many times.

He ate the last bite of stew with as much gusto as he had his first bite of food, then sat back, satisfied. He was glad for the teapot, which gave him a reason to linger. He savored his time, knowing that soon he would again be confined on a ship for another week. And after that, he had little idea of what to expect. He'd never attempted something like what Fallon had asked of him.

He couldn't let her down. It would mean letting the PAC down.

Nagali couldn't understand his affinity for the PAC, but Arlen did. Both of them, along with Omar, were prepared to help him get the job done.

They'd do it. Somehow.

He rejoined Omar and Nagali outside Docking Bay Eight. Arlen arrived last, looking tense. He wondered why. He was about to ask when a commotion erupted on the boardwalk. People were being shoved aside and shouts rose. Further down the corridor, Cabot saw security officers coming at a run.

He caught Arlen's eye. "This looks like the kind of thing you'd get involved in."

She cast him a long-suffering look, but his words sent her into action. Two men and a woman were at the center of the commotion, fast approaching. Arlen stepped out, prepared. Such a hero complex on that one. She really had missed her calling as a PAC officer.

As the trio rushed forward, Arlen stepped into the path of the one on the far right, snagging his foot as he ran and giving him a mighty sideways shove.

Omar Freeborn enjoyed few things as much as he loved a good brawl. The cause didn't much matter to him. He forged into the fray with a grin, taking down the larger man in a tangle of arms and legs and punches.

To Cabot's surprise, Nagali took advantage of the running woman's distraction. She swooped in and snagged her arm around the woman's neck yanking her back into a chokehold and forcing her to her knees.

Within seconds the security staff arrived, stingers in hand, pointed at the three. Omar was disappointed to relinquish his punching bag, but he did so, running a hand through his hair and smoothing his shirt.

"I suggest we leave now, before someone in security decides they want to debrief us for their records." Even Cabot would admit that sometimes, PAC processes could be exhaustingly tedious and inconvenient.

The four of them wasted no time boarding the *Outlaw*, requesting departure, and getting out of there.

Only once they got a safe distance away did Cabot relax.

He, Nagali, and Omar went to the mess hall while Arlen navigated the ship away from Blackthorn. None of them got any food or drink, but the mess was the only common space on the ship to congregate.

"That was pretty slick," Cabot said. "Taking down that fugitive."

Omar gave him a lazy grin. "Thanks. It was fun. Wonder what they did?"

Cabot shook his head, with a slight eye roll. "I didn't mean you. Your sister."

Nagali smiled, and it looked remarkably like her brother's grin a moment before. "Like I told you. I can do good things even when there's no profit in it."

"Right." Cabot didn't want to go back to that conversation. "So, I'm going to go up and see when Arlen can put us on autopilot. We need to work on the gratitude ritual. And start on the version of the goodbye ritual one uses when excusing oneself to the necessary, or other personal business."

Omar groaned. "Oh, you're just making shit up now."

"I assure you, I'm not. Since we'll be in close contact for an undetermined amount of time, it's one you'll need to know."

Omar made another sound of distress and defeat. "Is it too late to demand more money?"

"Yes." Cabot looked from him to Nagali.

"I'm not complaining," she said quickly. "I've already told you that I'm going to prove myself to you. To redeem myself." She lifted her chin in an uncannily heroic pose.

He suppressed a sigh. "I'll settle for getting this job done. I'll be back shortly, then we can get to work."

THE NEXT THREE days involved lessons for his three students all together, lessons for only Omar and Nagali, who would fulfill the attendant role, and lessons just for Arlen. Since Cabot would present her as his equal in these proceedings, she'd need to use the appropriate postures and responses.

"When in doubt, just maintain your posture and defer to me. That will seem normal to them, since I'm your elder," he told her. Rather than meet in the mess, they'd selected her quarters that morning as a change of pace.

She remained seated, holding her chest and shoulders up, her head tilted forward at just the right angle.

"Good." He approved of her diligent work.

"Are you sure Nagali isn't a more natural choice? I know Omar has to serve as your attendant, but Nagali is my elder too. And she's been quick to pick up the rituals."

Cabot sat on the bunk next to her. "She's smart, and she'll play her part well. But other than her sharp mind, Nagali's biggest talent is her charm. That won't work on Briveen. Nagali's biggest fault is her impetuousness. She makes quick decisions and throws herself into them. That is absolutely not what we need on this mission."

"She is charming," Arlen mused. "Sometimes I feel like she's a kindly aunt, who could be a close confidant." When Cabot opened his mouth to speak, she added quickly, "Of course I know better. I don't tell her anything I don't need to."

"She's dangerous like that." He knew only too well. "She can be almost intoxicating when she turns on the charm."

"It's impressive. I wish I had that in my arsenal."

He cast her a sidelong look. "You have your own qualities. You're upstanding and forthright. It's the opposite of her, but also effective. People know where they stand with you."

"She probably makes more money than I do."

"Maybe," he allowed. "But she makes more enemies, too. Her impulsiveness causes her to burn people."

"Like she did with you."

"I'm hardly the first person to be sacrificed for a Nagali Freeborn caper. It was foolish of me to think I was immune to it just because we were married."

She arched her back, stretching, and finally let her Briveen-friendly posture drop. "You were together more than ten years, right? That sounds like a pretty long run, for a capricious person."

"I feel like you're making a point, but it eludes me."

She smiled. "Not really. I was just thinking, if she's a scorpion, she's going to sting eventually. But imagine how much effort it took to wait that long to do it."

"Will it make you happy if I promise to think about it?"

"I wouldn't say 'happy.' I just think it's worth considering it from that perspective, if you never have."

He squinted at her. "You're the last person I'd have expected to stick up for her. Did she talk you into it?"

She shook her head with an exasperated expression. "Of course not. I mean, she probably would have, if she'd thought I was game for it. But I've been generally cold and standoffish with her. Seems like a good approach when it comes to her."

"That is a very strange paradox," he observed. "You represent her side of things, even though you don't like her."

"I didn't say I don't like her. I don't *trust* her. There's a difference. And I'm not saying this on her behalf. I'm saying it on yours."

He thought he knew what she meant, but wanted to be sure. "Why?"

"Because I think you've spent all these years stewing over it. And I think you'd be able to put it behind you one way or another if you really put yourself in her place to see it through her eyes."

"I'll think about thinking about it."

She shrugged, as if she didn't care either way. But if it didn't matter to her, she wouldn't have bothered to say anything. The whole thing left him feeling mildly disgruntled, and wanting to needle her just a little in return.

"Omar thinks you're cute. He's thinking about asking you out."

Yep. That did it.

"He's fifteen years older than me. No way."

"More than fifteen. But I thought I'd warn you." He smiled pleasantly.

She gave him a knowing look. "Sure you did."

"Well, you're talking about my former love life. I thought yours would be fair game. Since you wanted us to share such things. As friends do."

Her sour expression made him want to laugh.

She twisted her mouth, looking thoughtful. Then sighed. "You know, you're right. It isn't fair that I meddle in your affairs and never say anything about mine. The truth is, I don't date much. Pretty much never, actually. The kind of people I see on a regular basis are not the sort of people I want to date."

"Hmm. Men or women, or either?"

"Men."

He considered the problem. "So you like a kind of man you don't tend to interact with, in your life as a trader. Upstanding, right? Law-abiding." He rubbed his chin, thinking what her type would be. "But he'd have to have a sense of adventure and fun."

An image of Dragonfire's security chief appeared in his mind, and he examined it from all sides. It made perfect sense. He had remarkably good looks, an impeccable code of ethics, and a great sense of humor. Plus a uniform, which always held a certain attraction of its own, whether worn by a man or a woman.

"Arin Triss. It has to be," he declared. "But a security chief and a trader? Talk about unlikely pairings."

To his surprise, redness flooded her tanned face. Whoops. Apparently, she was more than just attracted to him.

It wasn't like Cabot to commit a faux pas, and he immediately felt contrite. "But," he said quickly, "opposites often attract, don't they? And you two are alike in the ways that would matter."

She ran a hand over her red cheek. "No, we're definitely not. What would we even talk about? It's just a crush."

He was certain it was much more than that, but he nodded agreeably. "We all have them from time to time. Even me."

That caught her attention. "Really? Who do you have a crush on?"

"No one at the moment. But when Captain Nevitt first arrived on the station, I couldn't stop looking at her."

The color in her face faded. "The captain? Seriously? Up until recently, she was made of stone."

"Yes, it was a short-lived attraction. But you can't deny, she's magnificent. She has this way of making you feel like she's deigning to talk to a mere bug. You know?"

She laughed. "And you find that attractive?"

"Of course." But he was smiling, making his answer ambiguous. "And you know what else?"

"What?"

"Don't tell anyone, but I think she and Ross Whelkin might be dating. Just a little. Very quietly."

"Really? Huh." Arlen tilted her head, probably imagining the two together.

Ross was part of Fallon's Blackout circle, having been an instructor of her team at the academy. The official story on Dragonfire, though, was that he was simply an intelligence officer.

But thinking of the formerly hard-as-nails workaholic Captain Nevitt dating Ross distracted Arlen sufficiently from her own romantic life, which seemed to be of the unrequited variety.

"We live in strange times," she finally said.

"That we do."

"So you'll think about the Nagali thing?"

"I will. If you'll think about asking Arin out when we return to Dragonfire." If she could poke at sensitive spots in the name of friendship, then so could he.

She gave her head a quick shake. "There's no reason for him to be interested in me."

That was entirely untrue. "Arin has gone out with just about every single woman who has come through Dragonfire. Why would you be the exception?"

"No, that's what I mean." Her mouth pulled downward. "He's one of the most popular people on the station. He's single and gorgeous, and I'm just...well, I'm fine, but not the sort of person that could hold his interest."

Cabot found no logic in her argument. "No one has held his interest thus far. And he's never so much as gone out with you. So isn't it reasonable to think that you might be different enough to be the one to hold his attention?"

Her brow furrowed and her look of confused surprise made him chuckle.

"See?" he said. "I'm making perfect sense. So if you'll think about asking him out, I'll entertain the idea that Nagali isn't an evil harpy."

She laughed. "I never said 'evil harpy.'"

"No. But I might have thought it a time or two, in the months immediately after our breakup."

"But not since?"

"Well...not very often since." He shrugged.

She laughed again. "All right. Deal. We can both do some thinking."

"Should we sign a contract?" he teased.

"I think a verbal agreement will do."

He left her quarters smiling.

Rule of Sales Number 9: Don't do business with friends or family.

Rule of Sales Number 10: Sometimes, you just have to ignore the rules.

On the way to relieve Omar of piloting duties, Nagali stepped from the mess hall, blocking Cabot's path.

His first instinct was to make a mildly sarcastic comment, but he curbed it. Instead, he looked at her through the lens Arlen had suggested. Had this woman fought to reign in her own instincts to be with him?

He tried to dismiss the idea as the idealism of a young woman who meant well. But he couldn't.

Nagali watched him, not saying a word as he squinted at her, trying to see her the way he had back on Dauntless. As a betrayer.

He shook his head and pushed past her.

Her hand on his shoulder made him pause.

"I'm not all bad," she told him. "I never was. I'm just not all good either. Or perfect." Her dark eyes pled for understanding, then she went back into her quarters.

Cabot looked toward the ship's tiny bridge, feeling conflicted.

It had been easier to simply hate her.

Ever since Arlen had raised the question, it had nagged him. He had to know.

Cabot rang the chime on Nagali's door, and it opened immediately. He didn't wait to sit, but dove right in.

"When we were together, did you force yourself to be the person you thought I wanted you to be?"

She'd painted her lips a deeper red than their natural shade, and the crimson color contracted. "No. I didn't. Well. Not exactly." Her eyes roamed the room as if she were casing it for a break-in.

After a long pause, she went on. "I would say I was ninety percent the real me."

"And the other ten percent?"

"I was making different decisions than I would have. Trying to be more…I don't know…reliable. Less…"

"Less Nagali Freeborn." Because she wasn't herself if she didn't fly by the seat of her pants, leaping from one fire to the next. What must that have been like for her?

"I'm sorry you felt you had to do that," he said.

She made a flicking gesture with her fingers. "It was nothing."

"It was."

She rolled a shoulder. "Okay, it was. But so what? I don't regret that choice. The times I spent with you were some of the best in my life. So far, anyway."

"But now I feel like I was…crushing your spirit or something."

Her bright lips pursed in amusement. "Do you really think that's possible?"

Okay, that was a dumb idea. Nonetheless. "How can you not regret all that time, being stifled?"

"I regret nothing of my life, except for one thing. The way that deal went with the medical supplies. Leaving you behind. You know I take risks. I gamble, and often I win big. On the occasions I lose, then I lose. The highs come with the lows. But I never meant to gamble with *you*. I really didn't."

"Then why didn't you ever track me down and tell me that?"

"Would you have listened?" she countered.

"No. But you could have made me listen, if you'd wanted to."

"I didn't track you down because you were right to leave. You were better off without me. I was bound to take another gamble sooner or later, and you could have gotten caught up in it. I didn't want that to happen."

She was right. And wrong, too. "You should have told me," he said quietly.

She raised her hands in a gesture that was half plea and half helplessness. "I couldn't, at that time. None of us are the same people we were a decade ago. Look at you. You're practically a diplomat."

"I'm not—" he said hotly, but she waved a hand.

"I mean no offense. I'm sure your business still has a sharp enough edge to draw blood. I just mean that the person you've become is not the same as the person you were."

He couldn't deny it. His life on Dragonfire had little in common with the life he'd led before.

"You're better," she pronounced. "And I'm better. *We* are better. Smarter. We know what matters to us."

"What matters to you?" he asked.

She smiled a familiar, sly smile. "The chase. The risk. And either the reward or the loss. Always that. But also, my brother. And you. Maybe even that hostile young protégé of yours." She laughed, a deep sound of delight. "She's something else. Not like us."

"I thought you'd hate her," he admitted.

"You don't know everything about me. I still have some secrets."

"Oh, I'm sure of that."

"Watch it." Her warning had no heat, though. "Arlen is the loyal sort. And she cares about you. So of course I like her. Don't tell her that, though. It would piss her off."

A new silence fell between them as they smiled at each other. It was a feeling of comfort.

It was strange.

"What do you plan to do after all this? I always pictured you married to one of those tycoons that owns his own little planetoid."

She waved her hand, dismissing the idea. "It was fun for a few months, but it got boring quick."

Was she serious, or just teasing him?

It didn't matter.

JUST AS CABOT reached the cockpit of the *Outlaw,* a sudden jolt threw him into the bulkhead. His shoulder took most of the force, and he managed to stay on his feet. Three more steps took him to Omar, cursing and hunched over the ship's navigation controls.

"Pirates," Omar barked without Cabot having to ask. "Maybe just some rippers who've gotten too bold. They're trying to disable us. I'm trying to keep them from it."

Omar did fine getting a ship from one place to the next, but he was no pilot, in the true sense of the word. Neither was Cabot.

Fortunately, Arlen barged in at a run. "Move!" she ordered.

Omar, looking like he couldn't decide between being peeved or amused, did as she said. He crowded next to Cabot, looking bewildered. It would have been funny in other circumstances.

"She's good," Cabot said to Omar, watching Arlen's hands fly over the controls, taking them into a steep bank and then a hard acceleration. The sudden force only lasted for a few moments, then let up just as abruptly. Cabot felt his guts try to force their way out of his middle, first on his left side, then careening across the front and his right. Then his back slammed into the bulkhead, much harder than his original jolt.

Omar dropped into the seat beside her, shrugging on the harness meant for hard maneuvers. Cabot followed suit, sliding his back toward the door until he reached an emergency panel.

He pulled it open and strapped himself into a harness, then activated the leg restraints.

He'd just secured himself when the ship inverted, a little too fast for the inertial dampeners to compensate. His stomach turned over and his equilibrium spun in a crazy whorl.

What was happening? He wanted to shout out a question, but didn't want to distract Arlen from piloting or Omar from the weapons systems.

"They're in range," Omar said. "Should I hit them?"

"No," Arlen bit out. "Wait."

A few more minutes of Cabot's innards trying to escape his body, and Arlen barked, "Prepare to vent plasma from the propulsion chamber."

Another session of spinning had Cabot wondering if internal organs could experience liquefaction.

"Now," Arlen ordered.

Cabot assumed Omar must have done as ordered, because the spinning stopped and after a sensation of fast acceleration, the pressure eased.

Arlen and Omar continued to stare at the voicecom display, making him think they weren't quite in the clear.

After several tense moments, the tension went out of them and they sagged in their seats.

"Can I ask now what happened?" Cabot didn't care for being in the dark all this time.

"They wanted to take our ship. Fortunately, that meant they didn't want to damage us too much. I outmaneuvered them, then vented the plasma right in front of their sensors, causing enough distortion for us to get out of weapons range. Turns out, we're faster than them, so they won't catch up to us."

"Why not disable them with weapons?" he asked. "This ship has lots."

"Weapons like this are above my pay grade," Arlen said. "I

have no experience with them. So I wanted to reserve all our energy for maneuvers, since I'm confident about those."

"Yeah you are." Omar gave her a gentle punch on the shoulder. "That was some fantastic flying."

She shrugged off the praise. "I do a lot of long-range runs. I have to be able to avoid trouble. The best way is always to just get away from wherever the trouble is."

She leaned forward to speak into the voicecom. "Nagali? Are you okay?"

After a long moment, Nagali's voice came through. "I'm fine. I think my arm's broken, though."

The three of them exchanged a look.

"Which one of us is most capable of handling a medical situation?" Cabot asked.

Silence.

"All right. Omar, let's go. Arlen, keep steering us away from people who want to shoot at us."

He removed himself from the harness and closed the panel that housed it.

"They didn't shoot at us," Arlen said, sounding like she was looking on the bright side. "Just a shaker charge to get info and cause mayhem."

"Steer us away from those, too."

"You bet." She seemed entirely too matter-of-fact. Did this kind of thing happen to her a lot?

He'd have to address that with her later. For now, he needed to look after Nagali. He grabbed an emergency medkit from the wall and headed for her quarters with Omar on his heels.

Her door wasn't locked, and when they entered, she sat gingerly on the edge of her bunk. Her wrist rested on the opposite knee, letting part of her forearm lay across her legs.

She'd understated the seriousness of the matter. Cabot saw two visible breaks, causing her arm not to form a right angle at the elbow, but hang in a dreadful "c" shape.

Cabot heard Omar come to an abrupt stop behind him.

"That's nasty." Omar's face paled and he put a hand to his stomach.

"Get out," Nagali told him, "before you throw up in my quarters."

Omar nodded and wheeled around, making a hasty exit. "Sure thing."

She smiled at Cabot. "He's always had a weak stomach for such things. Funny, since I've seen him break an arm or two over the years. Not his," she clarified. "Other people's."

"Right." Cabot kneeled on the floor next to her, taking a medical scanner from the kit and slowly guiding it through the air just above her skin. The device showed a great many readings, few of which Cabot could interpret.

"Well," he finally said, "it's broken."

Despite her situation, she laughed. It must have jarred her arm, because she winced. "You know, I had a feeling it was."

"I've never used a bone knitter. Have you?"

"A few times. For Omar. I'll guide you through it. But first you have to set the bone."

He really, really did not want to. But it had to be done. She'd be in misery if they didn't get the bones at least partially knitted.

"Okay. Fortunately, I do know what to do with this." He took an injector from the kit.

Nagali grimaced. "I hate those."

"I know. But I'm not about to touch that arm until your nerves are blocked."

"It won't be a simple nerve block. It will make me tired. And fuzzy." Her back straightened. "But do it."

He touched the injector to her upper arm, then the inside of her lower arm. Then he waited.

He gave her two full minutes before asking, "How are you feeling now?"

"Fuzzy at the edges. Loose." She let out a gusty sigh. "I hate it."

"Sounds like we're ready, then." He wanted to lie her down before setting her arm, but that would just hurt her more. So he gripped her wrist and bicep, then pulled the bones into place.

Even with the injection, she flinched and her other hand went to her face.

Supporting her arm with one hand, Cabot ran the scanner over it again. "I think that did it."

He put the scanner down and picked up the knitter. It was small and smooth. He guided it over her arm, back and forth, just like the first-aid classes taught. When the red light on the back of the knitter, lit, he stopped.

She was nowhere close to healed. She probably had soft tissue damage, but there was nothing he could do about that. She'd need to stay still until they could get to a medical facility. He sure wished a hospi-ship would wander across their path, but there'd be little chance of that.

He returned everything to the medkit and closed it. "That's all I can do."

She nodded once, her face full of fatigue. "Help me lie down?"

"Of course." He sat on the bed, then cradled the back of her head and her lower back as he shifted her to a reclining position.

She held her bad arm while he adjusted the pillow under her head.

"Better?" He was leaning over her, his hands at either side of her face.

"Yes. Thank you." Her voice was even deeper than usual, mix of rough and smooth that no one but Nagali could make possible.

Before he started getting nostalgic, he straightened.

"I think I'll sleep." She closed her eyes.

"That would be best," he agreed. "We'll check on you every hour or so, in case you need something. Try not to get up on your own."

"Okay." Her eyes opened. "Cabot?"

He turned back on his way out of her quarters. "Yes?"

"Thank you. For helping, and for hearing me out before. It's okay if you still hate me."

Her voice became increasingly soft as she spoke.

"I don't hate you," he said as her eyelids closed again.

As her door closed behind him, he heard a soft exhalation that sounded oddly like a smug "Hah." But it could have just been a sigh.

Even injured and sleeping, she had to be inscrutable.

THEY DIDN'T HAVE time to travel a day out of their way to visit a tiny PAC outpost, but they were lucky to be so close to one. After much deliberation, they'd decided that since the outpost offered both medical and mechanical services, they would gamble on the unscheduled tune-up giving them enough of a boost to compensate for the lost time.

Factoring into that decision was also the fact that arriving with a member of their delegation in poor health would reflect badly on them. It would reduce the likelihood of a successful negotiation.

Besides those factors, Nagali was in a lot of pain.

Outposts were nothing like stations. They were way stations, designed to assist travelers and ensure the upkeep of communications relays. They had no official names, instead being given alphanumeric designations. The PAC might as well have named them, since their crews and the travelers who frequented the outposts gave them nicknames anyway. Those nicknames were not always flattering.

The outpost that Cabot and his colleagues were fortunate enough to be near was known as Rusty. Never mind that the exterior of the station couldn't rust, in the absence of oxygen. Cabot did not find the name reassuring.

The staff was enthusiastic and friendly, though. Mostly young officers who hadn't yet started a family, and had to earn their stripes by taking on less desirable jobs, as was the norm for such places.

The outpost's doctor looked like he must have just earned his license. He met them at the docking bay and escorted Nagali to the infirmary himself. Cabot wondered whether it was good bedside manner, or just that the doctor had no other staff.

"Our mechanic will start right away on your repairs." The lieutenant in charge of Rusty looked to be in his mid-twenties, and either Zerellian or an Earther. It wasn't species-ist of Cabot that he sometimes found it hard to tell between the two groups of humans, since humans themselves had the same difficulty.

He continued, "You can wait in our mess hall, or we have a small common area. But you're more than welcome to hang out with us in ops control. It's nice to have some new blood around here to liven things up."

Cabot looked to Arlen and Omar, who both made small *it's fine with me if it's fine with you* shrugs.

Why not? It couldn't hurt to see if these PAC officers had anything interesting to say. They had a unique perspective, being stuck on their own out here.

They followed Lieutenant Davies through a passage so brief it barely qualified as a corridor. Likewise, ops control hardly looked like others of the name. It looked more like the cockpit of a tiny shuttle, with a jumble of control panels and devices crammed into too little space. Cabot eyed the floor-to-ceiling technology and spotted a couple switches on the ceiling. He wondered what those could be for.

"Thank you for inviting us up," he said to Davies and the ensign who sat at the science station. "It's nice to see some fresh faces after our travels, even though it's only been a couple weeks."

It was a mostly true statement, though it implied they'd been traveling straight through with no stops. But Cabot wasn't responsible for what the good lieutenant might infer.

He realized that he was, however, responsible for reporting this detour to Fallon. Or was it better not to send a message, to avoid possible interception?

No, this whole thing was her brainchild. She needed to know about it so she could fit it into whatever war-shaped puzzle she was trying to piece together. He'd just have to figure out a coded way to explain the situation.

Omar made introductions and they all exchanged polite PAC-approved bows.

"How have things been out here? I imagine it's been kind of rough." Cabot asked, employing sympathy and vagueness to draw out whatever was most on these officers' minds. It was a tactic that worked more than it failed.

The outpost hadn't furnished its ops control with many seats, as they'd take too much space. But Cabot didn't mind folding down an auxiliary jump seat and easing into it. He'd sat in worse accommodations, back in the day.

Arlen and Omar, being of Rescan sensibilities, opted to sit in jump seats along two other sides of the room, giving them all the greatest possible personal space.

"Well," the lieutenant said thoughtfully, "it's always something. But out here, we're kind of removed from everything, you know? We share this duty post in six-month rotations with a counterpart crew, and we're at the end of this rotation. In a week, we're headed to Jamestown. We'll get back in the loop then."

"For better or worse," Ensign Casey Ahra added, looking oddly chipper when making such a dire statement.

But it provided Cabot with a conversational opportunity. He nodded knowingly. "Are you thinking it will be worse? I've heard some troubling predictions."

Davies and Ahra exchanged a look.

Ah. Despite their warm welcome, these two wouldn't confide in them. It was like this sometimes. Some people, especially those within the PAC, thought little of Rescans. They judged them all by the worst-of-the-worst rippers.

"I'm sure everything will work out fine," Davies said with a smile. "The PAC will sort it all out."

"Of course." Cabot gave his most benignly pleasant smile. The smile he gave to customers in his shop who were obviously going to be impossible to please. "You know, I think I could do with some water. I tend to get a little dehydrated when traveling. All that recycled air, you know."

Davies nodded. "Oh, we know. There's biogel in the galley, right with the water. It's better for hydration."

Cabot gave the lieutenant an amused grimace. "That's true, though I've never cared for the taste. But I'm probably due for some."

"I think I'll join you." Omar stood.

"Arlen?" Cabot asked.

"I'm good. I'll stay here."

Cabot gave another of his pleasant smiles before leaving, with Omar in tow. Arlen was smart. She'd done as he'd hoped, remaining behind. Being closer in age to these two, she'd be more likely to get useful information.

In the mess hall, Cabot plucked a biogel from the cooler and sat with it. He did feel a little dry. He didn't, however, mind the taste of the hydrating drink. He downed it.

Omar, however, shuddered. "I hate that stuff, man. Don't know how you drink it."

"Yes, I seem to remember you dry-heaving once, when the choice was either biogel or severe dehydration." The mental image of big Omar, on his knees dry-heaving after drinking it, still amused Cabot.

Omar grabbed a bottle of water from the cooler and gestured with it. "I'm sick of people treating me like I'm a liar and a cheat just because I'm Rescan."

"To be fair, you are a liar. And a cheat."

"Only sometimes. In specific situations." Omar scowled, then downed some of the water. "Never with the PAC."

"And that's why you don't do all that much PAC business, right?"

"Whose side are you on?" Omar sent Cabot a hostile look, but it was blatant posturing. Cabot saw right through it.

"I'm just saying, there's a reason people think that. It's not always fair, but you know what? Sometimes it is."

"I guess." Omar reopened the cooler and poked around at the food. "Ah, meatballs. Nice."

"I don't recall them offering you their food," Cabot noted.

"They didn't say not to eat it, either. The way I figure it, they deserve for me to eat their food if they're going to assume I'm a bad guy."

Cabot smiled. "That's circular logic, isn't it? You're going to eat their food because they suspect you might be a ripper, but taking things that don't belong to you doesn't exactly dispel that notion, does it?"

"I'm just one guy, Cab. If I pulled out a kidney and offered it to them, they'd just think I was working some angle. So screw it. I'm going to eat all their meatballs." He dropped two packets into the heat-ex and slammed the door.

"All of them? I imagine they've got a pretty good supply."

"Every damn one," Omar confirmed. "Or as many as I can before the ship is ready."

Which proved to be a lot, but not all.

Two hours later, Arlen and a fresh and healthy-looking Nagali joined them at the docking bay. Cabot had already paid for the ship's maintenance and was more than eager to get back on their way at the greatest speed possible.

Once on board the *Outlaw,* he sent a message to Fallon.

"Just letting you know that the item you wanted had a slight defect. I've had it repaired, though it caused a slight delay. Hoping to make the time up en route."

Making it seem like she'd asked him to find a trade good for her seemed like a good cover. She'd figure out his meaning.

Given their proximity to Dragonfire, Fallon would receive the message in a matter of minutes.

"Did you send the message?" Arlen asked when he met her, Nagali, and Omar in the mess hall for a quick debriefing. Arlen had set the autopilot and they were hurtling toward Briv at the highest speed that wouldn't have the ship coming apart before they could arrive.

"Yes. Did you learn anything interesting on the outpost?"

"They're nervous." Arlen stood against the bulkhead, her arms crossed. "They just don't know if they should be more nervous about being on the outpost, or returning to Jamestown. I don't think they know more than we do. Actually, they probably know a lot less."

"Well, that doesn't tell us a lot, but it does tell us something. It means PAC command hasn't put auxiliary stations on high alert. That's a good sign." Cabot didn't take it as a great encouragement, but it was something.

Nagali, seated at a table, spoke up. "The doctor was a little more helpful. He said that his last shipment of medical supplies contained four times the normal quantities. In particular, he received medications used in treating deep-tissue trauma and radiation exposure."

They all looked at her.

"Why would he tell you that?" Arlen asked.

Cabot and Omar exchanged a knowing look.

"She has a knack for making people want to talk," Cabot explained.

Arlen's expression was dubious.

Nagali's lips twitched with amusement. "I did nothing untoward, I assure you. The doctor was just glad to have someone to talk to about such things. Seems his crewmates have no interest in his profession unless they're in need of his services."

"So PAC command is preparing its outposts, and presumably its stations and bases, to receive casualties. That's not promising," Omar mused.

"It's definitely not good news," Cabot agreed.

The other three wore brooding expressions, and he took it upon himself to boost their morale. "But we have a chance to make a difference, maybe turn the tide. So let's focus on what we need to do. Shall we work on the attrition ritual?"

"What should my face look like when we do that one?" Omar asked. "Should I look sorry?"

"Not sorry." Cabot shook his head. "It's attrition, not contrition. It's an acknowledgement of a breach of protocol, and the knowledge that it must be atoned for. Rather than being something emotional, it is an honoring of the social construct."

"What if I forget and I look sorry?" Omar wore a frown of uncertainty.

"Depends. If you're directing it toward me, that would be acceptable, since I am the one you're attending. If you direct it toward the Briveen, they will believe you are weak and that I should gut you."

"So I guess I'll just try not to look sorry." Omar smirked.

"Good plan," Arlen agreed.

"Okay. Let's go through it together, from the beginning." Cabot steeled himself for a long three days. It was cram time. If they didn't perfect everything, they could forget about success.

Cabot would not accept failure.

7

Cabot became so entrenched in the lessons that when Briv finally came into view on the *Outlaw's* sensors, it came as a surprise, like something out of context.

Or a bill he wasn't ready to pay.

They'd actually made it on time, in spite of everything.

But ready or not, the time was now. As Arlen docked the ship at the planet's orbital docking station, Cabot gathered the items he would take with them, and focused his thoughts. He mentally ran through the greetings, the words he would speak, and the negotiation itself.

The four went through the airlock, all wearing the cloaks of the Briveen business caste. Omar and Nagali, as the attendants, took the lead. They also carried the majority of items. The Briveen frowned upon using anti-grav carts for carrying luggage. That was what attendants were for. Omar looked a little amusing, carrying the large bag that held the scythe.

An orbital elevator had been held for their arrival, allowing them to board it right away and begin the descent.

During the hour-long ride down, Cabot continued running

through the coming events in his head while the other three occasionally exchanged observations.

As the orbital elevator settled at the transit station, Cabot closed his eyes and took a deep breath. He imagined himself in his shop on Dragonfire. In control. A master trader. Ready for any transaction.

They waited for the handful of other passengers to exit the elevator. Normally, on one this size, there would be dozens of people riding. Especially considering Briv had only two elevators. But few Briveen cared to leave home, and few offworlders visited because of the inherent difficulties in interacting with the Briveen. Instead of the traffic one would normally see at such a prosperous planet, most offworld transactions were arranged by proxy via the voicecom—usually in text-only messages. Deliveries and pickups happened en masse at the docking station, without requiring contact with the planet's surface.

Cabot shared a long look with Arlen, Nagali, and Omar in a moment of solidarity before embarking on this task.

Omar and Nagali led, with Cabot and Arlen lined up behind them. In tandem, their two attendants rolled their shoulders forward, ducked their heads, opened their arms wide, stepped to the right, then bowed. All the while, they kept their posture, shoulders, and head positions held just right.

Satisfaction and relief ran through Cabot's veins.

The Briveen attendants did the same, then all four attendants stepped to the side, allowing Arlen and Cabot to face the Briveen they would be working with.

They were not unfamiliar faces. In fact, they were so familiar that Cabot felt a tremendous flood of gratitude. Brak and Gretch were both frequent visitors of Dragonfire.

Regardless, the formalities had to be followed without fault. As the petitioners, Arlen and Cabot bowed. They performed the movements in tandem, just as the pairs of attendants had.

Only after they completed the sequence of postures and gestures did Cabot speak.

"I am Cabot Layne, of Dragonfire Station. I present Arlen Stinth, of the ship *Stinth*. Also, our attendants, who wish to express their gratitude at being in your presence."

Nagali and Omar performed synchronized bows, their eyes fixed on the two Briveen hosts.

The two Briveen performed the movements Arlen and Cabot had, but with far more grace and finesse. When they performed the ritual, it looked like a dance. Cabot had never engaged in such a formal encounter, and suddenly, the ceremony looked different to him. Not a stodgy clinging to tradition, but a celebration of life and unity.

Brak and Gretch combined slight head tilts to the side with a sweeping arm gesture, stepped back, and made a soft chirruping sound. Then they each turned clockwise in a full circle with their arms held to their sides, bent at the elbow, so that their hands were cupped toward the ceiling. They stepped forward, sweeping their arms ahead of them and holding them as if presenting a gift. Then they bowed. A chime rang behind them, struck by one of the attendants.

Cabot felt overwhelmed with the beauty and the feeling of ancientness.

The Briveen woman spoke. "I am Honorable Eighth Daughter Brak, of the House Grakaldi. I present to you the Honorable First Son Gretch of the House Arkrid. Also, our attendants, who wish to express their gratitude at being permitted to welcome such respected visitors."

All eight of them bowed again, a different bow with the shoulders rounded forward, to acknowledge the introductions.

"If you will permit us, we will show you to a meeting room so that our conversation may begin immediately." Brak tilted her head, and the light reflected off her blue-green, scaly skin.

"We would be honored," Cabot responded.

Two more attendants appeared, relieving Nagali and Omar of their luggage burdens. Omar retained the large bag with the scythe, while Nagali kept the bag containing the cat armor.

With a nod from Brak, the Briveen attendants led Omar and Nagali. Brak, Gretch, Cabot, and Arlen lined up side-by-side and followed behind, carefully ensuring that none of them stepped further ahead than the other. Good thing the corridors at the transit station were wide.

The Briveen attendants walked toward a room and the doors ahead whisked open. They entered, followed by Omar and Nagali. Then Brak and Gretch stepped in, followed by Arlen and Cabot.

He prepared himself for a great deal of such choreography.

Brak called the names of her attendants and dismissed them. After some bows, the attendants backed out of the room.

Brak let out a sigh and her posture softened. Cabot smelled the herbaceous scent of her relief.

"It's good to see you, Cabot." She smiled.

He appreciated her effort. Smiling wasn't natural for Briveen, and he knew she'd had to work at learning to do it. She and her people didn't have faces as expressive as the so-called "simian" species did. They were unique in their reptilian ancestry and used posture, hand gestures, subtle head tilts, and scent communication in place of facial expressions.

Which was no doubt how all these rituals got their start.

Gretch stepped in and offered his arm in a Rescan greeting. "I was glad when Brak told me it would be you. Fallon chose well."

Cabot grasped Gretch's arm at the elbow, feeling the cool synth-skin that covered the cybernetics. He had traded with Gretch many times. Occasionally for goods, but more often for information. Gretch was an ambassador for Briv, and often used Dragonfire as a way station.

Cabot didn't know Brak quite as well, though he'd become

better acquainted since the hospi-ship she lived and worked on, the *Onari,* had made Dragonfire its official home port. Brak had taken a leave of absence from her cybernetics work to visit home. Cabot was under the impression that it had been a long time for her.

Aboard Dragonfire, neither of these two engaged in the typical Briveen ceremonies. They preferred to follow the behavioral protocols of a PAC station. His familiarity with them didn't mean they'd be any more likely to agree to his—or rather Fallon's—plans, though.

"Brak, Gretch. It's a great pleasure to see you. I didn't realize you two knew each other," Cabot said, looking from one to the other.

"We didn't, until Fallon requested these negotiations," Gretch answered. "Funny that our paths never crossed on Dragonfire. I was put in charge of these talks, and if we come to an agreement, I'll be the one to present it to the council for final approval."

"They're too fancy to talk to you themselves." Brak's amusement wafted toward Cabot with the scent of sweet musk. "But Fallon mentioned to Gretch that I was visiting Briv, and since I have more knowledge of recent goings-on than most, he used his connections to get me assigned as his counterpart."

"You're too modest," Gretch chided. "That commendation you got from the PAC pretty much gave you access to anything you want."

"Tell my parents that," she said dryly. "The Briv government is crazy about me right now, but my parents are not. Especially my mother."

They made a fine pair. They were both taller than most humans, and even a little taller than most Rescans. Gretch's black-tinged, dark-green scales contrasted nicely with Brak's more iridescent ones. Cabot had considered matchmaking between them before, but had always stopped himself because getting involved in such things rarely paid off.

And now here they were, apparently getting along well.

Brak turned to Arlen. "I've seen you around. It's good to see you."

Arlen looked perplexed by the turn of events, and Omar and Nagali looked downright flummoxed.

Yeah, they didn't know what he'd been up to in recent years. They were beginning to get a sense of it, though.

Arlen gave a small Briveen bow of thanks. "It's good to see you too."

"We can dispense with the ceremonies and rituals," Brak told her. "Gretch and I are not traditionalists, and doing without them will greatly speed up our progress here."

"Really?" Nagali spoke up, sounding aggrieved. "After all the preparation we've done, I'm not sure whether to be relieved or annoyed."

Brak and Gretch laughed deep growling sounds of amusement.

Gretch nodded at Nagali. "I understand that. But believe me, by the time we got to the ceremony of accord and had to stare at each other without blinking for a full three minutes, you'd be wishing you'd never set foot on Briv. You'll still get a chance for some ceremony once your offering has been accepted by the council."

"You're probably right." Nagali looked at Gretch, a slow, seductive smile unfurling on her lips.

Cabot gave her a warning look and she reined herself in. The tightness in his chest loosened, thinking perhaps she would behave herself after all.

He couldn't resist a little salesman flair as he set the bag on the conference table. "I hope these items will be appreciated. I think we found something quite special." Rather than reach into the bag, he nodded to Omar.

Omar removed the scythe from the bag and put it on the table. "It's a scythe," he said.

Gretch touched the handle. Cabot had always wondered what kind of touch sensitivity Briveen had. Did their cybernetic arms and hands feel more than biological ones did, or less, or just differently? He'd never had a close enough relationship with a Briveen to ask such a personal question.

"What does it do?" Gretch asked.

"It's an ancient Briveen farming implement, for harvesting grain." Arlen looked anxious, perhaps thinking an unfamiliar item would be insufficient.

But Brak said, "How delightful. They'll definitely love this. One of our own historic artifacts, returned home. Nicely done."

"Ah, but there's more." Again, Cabot had a hard time repressing his showmanship. He gestured to the bag. "And it's even better."

He reached into the bag, extracting the box. Then he carefully removed the cat armor and set it on the table.

Gretch and Brak looked puzzled.

"It's armor," Omar said. "For a cat. You know. Cat armor."

Nagali rolled her eyes at him.

Omar was usually much smoother than this. The circumstances had clearly thrown him off his game.

"Why would someone need to armor a cat?" Brak asked.

"They wouldn't. That's the point. This is a Zerellian status symbol, from its colonial days. In perfect condition. Very rare."

Both Briveen now looked intrigued.

"Very interesting." Brak leaned down to peer at it closely. "It's masterfully made. I think it will be well-received."

Cabot tried not to feel smug. He didn't let that sentiment show, projecting only his pleasant sales persona.

Which he needed to quit doing. Briveen didn't need it. They could smell dishonesty or disingenuousness. On the bright side, their own irrepressible scent communication made them remarkably poor liars.

But then, what was a transaction without a little dishonesty? It felt somewhat like taking a bite of a ripe tango fruit only to find it had no flavor.

"I'm certain these will be accepted, and negotiations will be officially approved." Gretch ran a finger over the cat armor.

"Is there nothing else we can accomplish today?" Cabot asked.

"Officially, no. Unofficially, absolutely yes. Let's skip all the posturing and bluster, shall we? Tell us what's really going on." Brak sat at the table, indicating that the others should do the same.

Cabot felt a rush of gratitude that, in all this chaos and uncertainty, the right people had appeared. He felt like he'd been on a trapeze until this point, having let go, and flying through the air with his hands outstretched.

Now Brak and Gretch were catching him.

Maybe together, the six of them could actually make this happen.

CABOT HAD to walk a careful line. He could be as transparent with Brak as he could with anyone, given her relationship to Fallon and the depth of her knowledge of current, hidden, events within the PAC. However, Nagali and Omar sat at the table with them, listening to every word. Cabot was certain Fallon would not want them hearing what he was about to say.

He wished he could send them out to do some task, but he had no reasonable job he could assign them to assist his subterfuge.

His only option was to be blunt. "The information I'm going to relay is of a sensitive nature, and I'm under orders to reveal it only to specific individuals. As such, I'm required to ask Nagali and Omar to remove themselves." He looked to Gretch. "Could they be shown to their guest quarters, for a chance to relax? We've been working hard, on a tight deadline, and they could use some leisure."

His explanation was mostly truth, with a little embellishment. The best and most convincing lies were based in truth.

Omar appeared to be just fine with the idea. Cabot imagined he'd be perfectly happy to avoid the talking part of this venture. Nagali, on the other hand, looked mildly annoyed, though she tried to cover it.

She hated being left out of anything.

"Of course." Gretch touched a voicecom panel on the table in front of him. "Someone will be here momentarily to show them the way."

Cabot took the opportunity to give them a reminder. "Remember all the things I taught you about interacting with Briveen and follow them to the letter. Others are not as flexible as our friends here."

Brother and sister exchanged a long-suffering look, and Cabot pretended not to notice. It didn't matter whether they objected to his reminder or the content of it, so long as they did as instructed.

The doors whisked open and, after some dutiful bowing and posturing, the Briveen attendants showed Nagali and Omar out.

"So, what's going on?" Brak looked from Cabot to Gretch and back again. "Gretch has convinced me that we can trust him, so you can speak freely. I believe my people deserve to have a representative who understands what's really in play here."

If Fallon trusted Brak, and Brak trusted Gretch, that was good enough for Cabot.

"Right." He noticed how skeptical Arlen looked and patted

the back of her forearm in reassurance. "I'll preface by saying that I'm not privy to minute details of the events that have occurred in past months. You, no doubt, have seen a portion of these events unfold in a way that I have not. Just as I've seen them from my own perspective. So keep that in mind. I'm not asking to be filled in on what you know. If Fallon wanted me to know, then I already would, and when it comes to BlackOps intelligence, I make it a point to avoid knowing things that might get me in trouble."

He smelled sweet musk, mixed with anise. He imagined the musk came from Brak, while the anise indicated Gretch's worry. He felt a little sorry for Gretch, who was embarking on more than he realized.

Brak said only, "I understand. Please continue."

"The Barony Coalition's ambition has overflowed. They are aware that the Jamestown disaster was not the controlled exercise in caution the PAC claimed it to be. During the power struggle, a few treaties were violated and they know that. How much they know isn't clear. But by their actions, they've already relinquished their trade membership in the PAC. Fallon believes they're using the non-PAC worlds that are part of their coalition as a launching pad to escalate matters."

"And she believes they're headed our way," Gretch surmised. "Which explains why Barony keeps incurring on our space, in spite of our warnings. They're testing us."

"Yes. Briv would be a tactical coup, both for location and technological production. Fallon believes you're likely to be their first big stop."

"What's the plan?" Brak asked.

"Simple. You promise to immediately swing your production toward manufacturing as many ships as you can for the PAC. In return, they will offer protection far above and beyond the stipulations of your PAC membership. A constant presence around Briv, and a small ground force as well."

"Do you mean we would be required to cancel all current production contracts?" The set of Gretch's shoulders showed his tension.

"Yes." Cabot plunged on. "I know that's problematic, both because of economic ties and honor. This plan minimizes the economic impact, and isn't survival more important than honor? Honor can be redeemed, but lost lives cannot."

"You're assuming Barony would go that far," Gretch argued. "Maybe they won't, and we'd have damaged our business relationships for no reason."

"The Barony Coalition hasn't sacrificed its trade ties with the PAC for no reason. They must have a very big plan in mind. And think about it—where would they go first? What planet would be the most strategic? They don't need food—the PAC planets are the ones at the disadvantage there."

"Sethanos would be a prime target." Gretch looked thoughtful. "They have several planets rich in minerals, and a couple of them aren't even inhabited. Having those mineral resources would be an asset to them in a war situation."

"And they could put those minerals right into production here on Briv," Brak added. "He's right. We are very attractive, strategically. Regardless of whether we're their first target or second."

Gretch clacked his teeth in agitation. "That's true. But how am I supposed to present this to the council? They don't have the insider information that you do. All they have to judge by is some hostile behavior by Barony that hasn't amounted to anything. The council might not think the situation is dire enough to accept."

Cabot smelled anise, but a calm settled over him. He didn't share Gretch's worry. "This is a deal that both sides need. The PAC is already committed, so we're already half done. What's left is to sell it to your superiors. And selling is what I do best."

Gretch looked to Brak as if seeking confirmation. He must

have been satisfied, because he pushed back from the table. "Then the first step is for us to present your gifts to the council, who will decide if they are acceptable. If they approve, the negotiations officially begin."

Brak stood. "They're fine gifts, in my opinion, but what do you think the council will say?"

Gretch tilted his head thoughtfully to the side. "They're perfectly acceptable gifts if they want to accept. I shouldn't say that, but it's true. The only question is whether they wish to hear what our visitors have to say, or attempt negotiations."

"Knowing what you do of them, do you believe that to be likely?" Cabot asked.

"I can't say. They've surprised me before. Probably because they know about internal affairs I am not privy to. And sometimes, our xenophobia gets the best of us, as a people. But I think the proconsuls will like your gifts."

"So it's the proconsuls that are the most important to impress," Cabot surmised.

"Yes. The council will generally go along with the proconsuls. Those two are…what do you traders call it, the person you're targeting…your mark?" Brak looked at him for verification.

A pair of planetary leaders described as marks? He had to fight back a chuckle, as Brak might take it the wrong way.

"You could say that," he agreed. "The good thing is that I think they already know they need the PAC's assistance. That's most of the pitch right there. All we have to do is convince them that the price they're being asked to pay is worth it. Time is our enemy, though. Each day that goes by without a Barony attack makes the next day more likely to be the day they hit the PAC with a blow we might not recover from. Whether that first happens here or on Sethanos or somewhere else entirely."

Gretch clacked his teeth. "Hopefully we can get them to

approve the gift today, so that we can arrange a meeting for you with the council tomorrow."

"Better if it were today," Cabot said, "but I'll work with whatever I can get."

"We'll do all we can," Gretch assured him.

"Be sure to use that commendation of yours to full advantage," he advised Brak, wishing he could be there to hear the conversation among the council and proconsuls. He admired how Brak had leveraged the help she'd given the PAC into an official commendation.

"I will," she said. "But in spite of my present popularity with my leaders, I have no actual position with the government. I'm only here because my current status as a celebrity is beneficial to them. Gretch is the one with an actual position here."

"A commendation from the PAC is as high an honor as it gets," Gretch pointed out. "You can't blame the council for using that prestige for their own advantage. I've seen them make a big deal over far less." He turned to Cabot. "While you wait, you and your friends might enjoy the museum we have right here at the station. It has a great many Briveen artifacts and art pieces. I'd be surprised if your scythe didn't find its way there. I don't recommend leaving the station without escorts, though. Most people will be perfectly friendly, but every now and then there's a jerk. If they chose to confront you and it got reported to the council that you'd been involved in a confrontation..."

"It would reflect badly. I get it. But anywhere on the station is okay?"

"Yes. We have cameras and security in all common areas. You'll be quite safe, and even if someone bothered you, the instigator would be obvious, and that person would suffer a great dishonor."

"I see. So the jerks only act like jerks when nobody's looking." Cabot probably shouldn't be amused by that, but jerks were jerks anywhere you went—that didn't change even on a planet as unique as Briv.

Brak reached for the scythe, removed it from the bag, and held it against her shoulder.

"You're going to carry it like that, out and exposed?" Gretch's growl of amusement, in turn, amused Cabot.

Brak chuckled. "I figure if I'm going to carry an ancient farming tool, I might as well look cool doing it."

Brak indeed looked fearsome with her height, muscular physique, and such a primitive weapon.

Cabot looked to Arlen, who smiled. She was beginning to like Brak, he was sure.

"All right then," Cabot said. "As unlikely as it might seem, we will do some sightseeing while we wait to save the galaxy."

Brak and Gretch led the way to the door.

"That's a little melodramatic, don't you think?" Gretch asked.

"Is it?" Cabot lifted an eyebrow.

"Maybe not." Gretch's jaw tightened as if fighting the impulse to clack his teeth in annoyance.

Cabot stood next to Nagali as they looked at an ancient Briveen battle helm. Whoever had worn it had seen some hard times, judging by the large dents in it.

"I like this better than the art," she said. "Real items used by real people. They have their own stories and mystery."

He'd tried several times to move ahead with Omar or Arlen, but somehow Nagali kept ending up next to him. Looking at him with her big, inky eyes and her flirtatious, knowing smiles.

It was maddening. He was determined not to let it show, though.

"I agree." He kept his voice blandly neutral. "Personal items like this certainly make me think about the people who used them, and what may have happened to them." He moved on to the next display, which held a handmade stone ritual kit. "But look at this. It's art. Can you imagine making a bowl of out stone, and polishing it to a shine like that? That took great skill."

"It's lovely," Nagali agreed, looking at the set. "But this isn't art for the sake of art. It was used for ceremonies that were considered crucial to their civilization. That makes it a survival tool."

They moved on again. Cabot gestured to a four-meter by three-meter painting of a battle. "But what about this? This shows something about the people who made it, in that particular point in time when they made it. It shows what they valued, and what they found noteworthy for public remembrance. That's thought-provoking too."

"I suppose." Nagali didn't look convinced. "Sometimes I think museums like this are a shame. Think how much the government could get for these pieces, which serve no purpose but to be looked at."

"You really see no purpose in these people honoring their ancestors and remembering their history? Or of sharing it with offworlders like us?"

She sighed. "I get it. I just can't help seeing the missed opportunity. An item that just sits around doing nothing but existing, and is worth lots of money, well, it makes me itchy."

He couldn't help chuckling. "I think in the old days, you'd have been one of those tomb-raiding adventure rogues. The kind that always gets shot in the end."

"If I'd been a tomb-raider, I definitely would not have gotten shot. Only a very bad thief gets killed."

"Is there such a thing as a good thief?" he wondered.

"If you're the one getting robbed, no. But if you're very, very good at what you do..." she winked at him.

Sometimes he had a hard time telling if she was teasing or serious.

Arlen joined them, with Omar trailing her. Though he'd suggested a romantic interest in Arlen, he'd been nothing but pleasant and friendly, and Cabot was glad for that. He didn't need any drama developing between the two. Not while they had work to do here.

"What do you think of the museum?" Cabot asked Arlen.

"I think it's fascinating."

A high-pitched child's voice interrupted. "Look mama, those people are all smooth."

Cabot turned to see an embarrassed Briveen woman shushing one of the three children with her.

"Children make their own rules." Cabot gave the woman a polite bow and a gesture that meant he took no offense.

He pretended not to notice her obvious surprise at his knowing how to handle the situation. "Your children are observant, and look very strong."

Complimenting a person's children was universal. Cabot knew of no people who failed to respond well to it. Though the Briveen's preference for praising strength and health was a little different than some.

"You are kind to notice." The woman bowed. Her scales were a light, yellowy shade of green that Cabot hadn't seen before. They were lovely.

Two children had scales like their mother, while the outspoken one had a darker monochrome green. All children were adorable, but Cabot found Briveen children especially so. This was his first time seeing them in person, and was charmed by how boisterous and improper they were, compared to their elders.

As the family moved away, the child that had spoken turned back to watch them. To him, Cabot's group must look very strange.

The child gave Cabot a surreptitious wave with his three-fingered, biological hand before they turned a corner and moved out of sight. He wouldn't receive his cybernetic replacement arms until he turned eighteen.

"I can't imagine having one kid, much less three." Arlen shook her head. "Briveen moms must have incredible patience."

"Having clutches of three or four is normal." Cabot led his little group to an art installation in the middle of the room—a forged-metal freeform design. He had no idea what it was. "I guess it's all a matter of what you're used to."

Only the highest caste of Briveen was permitted to have children. A thousand years ago, Briveen had suffered a high rate of genetic mutations that had affected their ability to have healthy children. For the survival of their species, they'd begun requiring proof of genetic health before approval to have a child. Infant mortality plummeted, and the tragedy of dead children stopped. Over time, with greater scientific knowledge, the Briveen had perfected their ability to produce healthy children and prevent fatal mutations.

Cabot wasn't going to explain all that now. It wasn't the place, and chances were, his companions already knew. They should, if they'd done their homework, and if they hadn't, then they weren't very good traders.

The rest of the museum was a randomly-placed collection of armor, weapons, food implements, and art. Cabot could find no explanation for this choice of design. Most museums sorted items by type or by time period.

What did it mean? He wondered about it as they walked to the quarters they'd been assigned. Omar and Nagali led, as they'd been there before.

"Don't you love the architecture and design here?" Arlen asked. "They're so deceptively simple."

Nagali half-turned to shrug at her, wearing an indifferent sneer.

"It's nice," Omar said, rather lamely.

Arlen looked to Cabot.

He said, "Yes, I've been admiring it too. There's an organic flow in the subtle color gradations and subtle changes in texture and thickness. This entire transit station is a masterpiece in understated, perfected beauty."

Arlen brightened, glad someone else saw what she did. "Exactly. The materials are neo-industrial, but the style is something else."

"I've never seen anything like it." He hadn't even noticed at first, when he'd been focused on Brak and Gretch and the job ahead. Now, he scrutinized everything, recognizing the complexity of making it all so deceptively simple.

It was breathtaking.

It meant something, he was certain. But whatever the meaning was, Cabot was missing it. He felt it like a presence, hovering just out of his reach. His nose itched something fierce.

He declined an invitation to join the others in the quarters shared by Nagali and Arlen. He wanted to be alone in his own room to think.

The answer was right here, in this transit station, and he needed to figure it out.

Briveen brandy wasn't much like Alturian brandy, but it would do the job. Cabot sat in the silence of his quarters—which were decorated in the same elegantly simple style as the rest of the station, creating a quiet sophistication that suited him remarkably well. He'd decorated his own quarters on Dragonfire in a similar way, with clean lines and no clutter.

"There's something to that..." he muttered, swirling his brandy in its bulbous little glass. "But what?"

Something at the edge of his thoughts evaded him; something about how to present the deal to the Briveen that would allow them to accept it, giving both them and the PAC what they needed. Something simple. Pragmatic.

Yes, that was it. Something pragmatic. Only a highly pragmatic species would create a caste system that allowed for the continuance of their species. Or adopt the practice of having their short arms removed at the age of eighteen so they could be replaced with strong cybernetic ones that better suited the rest of their powerful bodies.

But then, their devotion to ceremonies and rituals did not seem so pragmatic. They were a time-waster, really. Cabot had a theory about that, and he wanted to talk it over with an expert.

He set his glass on the table in front of him and leaned forward to touch the voicecom display. He opened a channel to Brak, but she didn't answer. She might still be with Gretch and the council.

"Brak, when you get this message, I would appreciate it if you could come to my quarters. I need to discuss something with you."

He picked up his glass and sat back, swirling the brandy again. He did more swirling than drinking, as he'd never been a heavy drinker and the Briveen brandy felt like it was strong enough to use in place of orellium in a ship's propulsion chamber.

He sat, thinking of every transaction he'd ever conducted with a Briveen, and everything he'd ever read or heard about them. The solution he was reaching for could be hiding in the recesses of his experiences.

When the chime sounded, he checked the tiny camera on the doors to make sure it was Brak before he answered. He didn't need an encounter with Nagali right now. But it was Brak, so he put down the glass and greeted her.

"Thank you for coming so quickly," he said.

"I came as soon as Gretch and I finished with the council."

"How did that go?"

"Fine. They accepted the gifts. They have agreed to hear your proposal at noon tomorrow." She remained standing, as he hadn't yet invited her to sit. But he had other plans, if she agreed to them.

"I'd hoped for early morning. Time is slipping by too quickly."

"Then we should figure out your strategy. What can I help you with?"

He appreciated her directness. "Have you ever heard of 'the nose?' As in, a Rescan trader having a good nose for business."

"I don't know that I have." Her tone suggested she was puzzled by his topic change.

"It's a certain business sense. It's something I've always honed. Almost like an additional sense—the shrewdness of sensing a shift in markets, or an opportunity that is not readily apparent to others. Rescans value the nose greatly."

"Okay. But I don't understand how that relates to me."

He continued, "My nose tells me there's a solution here, right in front of me. I'm just not seeing it. I'd like to talk to you about your people, if you wouldn't mind, to see if I can get that solution to come into focus."

"Of course."

"And, if possible, I'd appreciate going outside of this station and seeing a bit of Briv while we do it." That was the tricky part, and he watched her closely.

"That's fine. But just you, and you need to stay right with me."

"I wouldn't dream of wandering off." He didn't need a

conservative-minded Briveen cracking him upside the head with one of those powerful cybernetic arms.

"Very well. When would you like to go?"

"Now. I feel like there's no time to waste."

"Is there anything particular you'd like to see?" Brak asked.

They'd just cleared the exterior doors of the transit station and Cabot drank in his first in-person view of Briv.

It was beautiful.

He'd seen green planets, but Briv put even Sarkan to shame. In one glance, he saw a greater variety of trees than he'd ever seen in one place. Most were shades of green, but there were some yellows and reds too. Smooth bark, spiky bark, and every texture in between covered the tree trunks that reached toward the sky. Flowers, shrubs, and tall decorative grasses grew full and vibrant along every pathway and sidewalk. The temperature was a few degrees warmer than the warmest spring day on Rescissitan. The sky was a brighter color, too, with a hint of green hidden within the blue. It added to the lush, verdant quality.

And the smell. The air was clean and lightly scented with floral and herbaceous notes.

"By Prelin, this is incredible. The voicecom images don't even begin to do it justice."

Brak concealed her amusement well, but he sensed it.

Quickly, he answered the question he'd ignored. "I didn't have anything particular in mind. I just want to see life. I'd never even seen Briveen children before today. I'd like to better understand your people."

"Let's walk down the main avenue, then." She started forward and he kept as close as he comfortably could. Briveen needed less personal space than Rescans, and he tried to split the difference. "Just remember to let me lead any interactions with others."

"Of course."

"We do have a handy trick to sidestep obligatory greetings and rituals. When walking in public like this, it's perfectly polite to avoid eye contact."

"Really?" He was intrigued. "I've been told that failing to maintain eye contact with a stranger is insulting."

"That's true, but since we cross paths with a lot of unfamiliar Briveen every day, we have to have workarounds. Otherwise, we'd never get anything done."

They walked slowly by a square with a fountain, where children ran and laughed and squealed.

"You avoid stopping for greetings by pretending not to notice one another."

"Yes." She led him further down the avenue, and they passed doctors' offices and storefronts.

"Wouldn't it be easier to shorten the rituals? Just turn it into a '*hello*' and a nod, like most species?"

"It would, and teenagers tend to push their limits by behaving like the simian species. I think eventually, gradually, we'll get to that point. But for now, we just politely ignore one another."

Cabot chuckled. One species' politeness was another species' insufferable rudeness. He loved the variety of it all. "So why have the rituals? I know it's tradition, but why hang onto such ancient ways?"

"You'd be surprised how long-lasting the effects of near-eradication of your species can be. It became ingrained in us that we would continue only if we adhered to our castes. The rituals helped define the castes. The castes shaped our government and our way of life. So you see, it was a circular process, one thing reinforcing the other. And underneath it all was the memory of nearly going extinct due to our own genetic failures."

Cabot could see how that would put great pressure on a people. "But technology and medicine have come so far. Gene therapy and genetic screenings would permit all people to have children, if they chose. People wouldn't be limited in life due to their genetics."

"Would you believe that it is we of the illustrious breeding caste that, in fact, have the greatest limitations? When we are born and certified as genetically healthy, our future as breeders becomes a matter of national pride and survival. We're the 'nobles,' the highest caste, and we're essentially forced into slavery." With a look of chagrin, she corrected herself. "I shouldn't have said that. Not slavery. It's just…a terrible duty, if it's not what you want."

"I see," Cabot said softly. He understood her better now.

She cleared her throat and continued in a lighter tone. "To escape it isn't easy."

"But you did. And now you've come home a hero. Things like that help create change, don't they? To help society pioneer new ways that better serve it?" A Briveen couple passed them, resolutely ignoring their existence. He and Brak returned the favor.

"Yes. And you're right," she answered once the others had passed. "I do hope I can be an example for others, to effect change. The council has been remarkably supportive. I was surprised. I think they're more eager for change than the general public. I suspect they're doling out as much progress as they believe the people can handle."

Cabot stopped walking. "Now that is fascinating." Then he hurried to catch up to Brak and match her pace again. "Would you say that the council is hoping we'll come up with a proposal they can accept without the citizens of Briv expressing outrage?"

"I can't speak for the council. My interaction with them is limited to the past weeks since my return. But from what I've observed, and from what Gretch has said, yes, I believe that's probably so."

"Then it isn't truly the council we need to sell our proposal to, but all Briveen."

"I think that's fair to say," she agreed.

"Hm." That gave him more food for thought, but still wasn't quite the angle he was grasping for.

She stopped in front of a narrow gray building. "Let's go in here. I want you to try something."

The building maintained the simple-but-elegant esthetic he'd noted at the station. Everything did, really. The lush greenery wasn't overly manicured, but he saw no weeds, either. There was no crowding, no gaudiness of having signs slapped everywhere the eye looked. The architecture of the buildings varied somewhat, but they all blended together.

"There's something almost Kanaran about how well everything goes together here. There's a sort of harmony to all of it. Would you agree?"

She paused, with one hand poised to pull an old-fashioned manual door handle. "When you put it that way, I can see a similarity. I've visited Kanar many times. Their buildings and art look harder, with a strong emphasis on thick, straight lines. At least that's how they look to me. But the colors and styles of buildings and roads match one another, so I see what you mean."

"You don't see hard lines here?" He gazed at his surroundings, trying to see what she saw.

"Not really. I see gentle curves and slopes. Gradual arcs. Like the architecture isn't in a hurry to get anywhere, and it isn't determined to aggressively pit itself against everything in its vicinity either." She chuckled and finally opened the door. "If that doesn't sound crazy."

"It doesn't," he assured her. "Not in the least."

Once inside, Cabot took in his surroundings. "You thought I needed to see a mandren meat store?"

Shanks of raw meat hung behind the counter in a see-through cooler. Smaller cuts were displayed within a case. Behind the display, a Briveen stood.

"Thank you for entering my shop. How may I help you today?" he performed a bow and three hand gestures that were an odd mix of a brief introduction and a gratitude ritual, but both vastly abbreviated.

Brak made a single gesture and a simultaneous bow, which seemed like an abbreviation for a return introduction. Very interesting. "We'd both like a stick of smoked mandren jerky. Sweet citrus glaze, I'm thinking."

Cabot tried to hide his horror. He'd smelled the mandren meat on Dragonfire, and he had no interest in repeating that olfactory experience, much less put a piece of the large game rodent into his mouth.

"Trust me." Brak smelled of sweet musk, and he was glad she was amused rather than offended by his reaction.

Did Briveen play practical jokes? Perhaps that was his next lesson.

The man behind the counter straightened, having bent at the waist to reach into the back and extract two sticks with brown meat skewered onto them. Brak used the proferred infoboard to transfer the cubics.

"Thank you." She bowed, but did nothing more.

The mandren meat seller returned the bow, and that was it.

They exited the store, each now holding a stick of jerky. It had a thick orange sauce on it that made Cabot even more wary.

"I somehow thought transactions like that would be far more difficult here. Greeting Briveen on Dragonfire requires a great deal more effort than what you just did."

She chuckled and continued on their previous path, walking down the avenue. He fell into step beside her.

"We're held to a higher standard elsewhere. We always err on the side of formality, because honor is important. If someone were to streamline with someone when we should have been formal and that person took offense, word could get back to someone who would care, and it could cause embarrassment. Embarrassment is not suffered well among my people. But when we've met someone before, and we've both agreed to minimize rituals, we can informally streamline. Now, if the proconsul had been in the store, we'd have all performed every full ritual, beginning to end, no exceptions."

"So, do most people streamline, as you call it?"

"It's hard to say, since you only do it with people you're familiar with. So I don't know how others act when I'm not around. But in my experience, people of my generation tend to prefer the quick versions. People of my parents' generation are about half and half. Some more relaxed, and some more formal. My mother, as an example, is relentlessly formal."

"That must be hard," he said carefully.

"It's a lot more than that. She's as old-fashioned as it gets. If she hadn't been that way, I might not have been forced to leave home for all these years."

"This is your first time back? How long were you gone?"

She was quiet for a long moment before answering. "Since my eighteenth birthday."

"Wow."

"Yeah. I missed being here. Even missed my mother, though when I left, I was sure I never would. But home is home. And your parents are your parents. She isn't a bad person, she's just...very traditional."

"So that commendation was your shot at redemption. What does she think of it?"

"It got me in the door, but only because everyone else is

impressed enough to ignore my running away. What other people think matters a great deal to her."

It was hardly a Briveen-exclusive trait. Cabot had known many people who put great stock in the opinions of others. He had never much liked that sort, but he didn't say as much to Brak.

"When she sees how much people respect your work, and how well you served the PAC, she could become more accepting."

"Maybe."

Their conversation lulled, and he could no longer forestall the meat stick in his hand. Brak took a bite, chewed, and nodded to him. "Go ahead."

He gathered his nerve, and his guts, and lifted the stick to his mouth. With the feeling one might have when being launched out of an airlock, he bit and chewed.

Smoked, spiced meat and a thick, sweet sauce flooded his taste buds. The flavor was somewhat like barbeque but without the acidity.

"It's good." He couldn't keep the surprise out of his voice.

Brak laughed. "Next time, just trust me. Mandren jerky is very different than mandren steak. The cooking process takes out all the gaminess."

Amazingly, he took another bite, and then another. Soon, he held only a stick.

"Next time, I'll trust you," he promised as she tossed them into a recycling chute discreetly located on the side of a building. He hadn't noticed it there until she opened it.

"Is any of this helping you at all?" she asked as they continued to stroll.

"I don't know. I haven't been struck by a sudden epiphany thus far, but that doesn't mean I haven't found what I need. I might just need a little time to make the connection."

"So this *'nose for business'* is a particular kind of intuition?"

"Yes, that's it exactly. Intuition, based on experience and the rules of business."

"There are rules?" She tilted her head curiously.

"Not officially. They're my rules. Rules I've developed over time."

"Like what?" she asked.

"Like Rule of Sales Number Eleven: Share what you know if it might get you what you need, but keep some secrets for yourself."

"I'm trying to decide if that's actually a rule, or if you just said that to pacify me."

"Why can't it be both?"

She chuckled. "I can see why Fallon likes you."

"I'll take that as a compliment. And I could say the same about you," he added.

"Then I'll take it as a compliment as well."

They walked in silence for several more minutes, giving him an opportunity to surreptitiously watch the people he was pretending not to notice.

"What else can I show you?" she asked. "I'm not sure how to help. And I don't want to take you somewhere that we'd have to observe all the proper rites. I get enough of that as it is."

"Do other people feel that way, do you think? That they are so reluctant to perform the formalities that they just avoid going places?"

"Sure," she said. "Doesn't everyone? I mean, haven't you ever wanted to go down to the boardwalk to get something, but didn't want to have to put on proper clothes and comb your hair?"

"Once or twice."

"It's the same thing. Cultural expectations can be more than you want to deal with. Everyone works around it as best they can."

"Now that is a fascinating observation. And astute." He

would have to give that some serious thought. "What else might I be surprised to know about Briveen?"

"We like to make dark jokes, often involving killing others in graphic and imaginative ways. I've found out firsthand that other species can find this disturbing. I have to be careful about that."

"I did know that," he said. "I do some trade with Honorable Hrekk of the house Grikkod, and he likes to try to surprise me with his jokes."

She made a click of sympathy. "Last of his line. It's sad."

"Does that have to do with genetics?"

"Yes. It doesn't happen often, but some of those recessive traits are hard to shake. Even a genetically healthy woman may be unable to have children. Or she might only have one clutch. Or have multiple clutches that never hatch. That's why it's important that all healthy females do have children."

Cabot tried to imagine that. "That's got to be a lot of pressure. Being forced to choose whether to have children for the future of your people, or to follow your own dreams."

"Yes. I used to wish I'd been born defective so I could become a scientist and stay here on Briv. But I'm 'lucky' enough to have been born to the most reproductively successful house on the planet. Almost all of us are genetically healthy. Plus, we tend to have large clutches with few bad eggs."

She said it all nonchalantly, but it made Cabot sad. There was something tragic about the Briveen arranging their entire society toward the goal of not dying out.

"Have advances in science helped with that?"

"Yes. More and more. Hopefully, one day, it will stop being an issue entirely. But for now, it's still difficult for creatures of our complexity to reproduce via eggs. Without our scientific acumen, we'd have died out long ago."

They fell silent. Apparently, talking about an entire species' difficulties in sustaining itself and the ways it affected its members was a conversation killer.

Brak lifted a contrite shoulder. "I've depressed you. I'm sorry."

"No, there's nothing to be sorry for. There's a reason this isn't something that people normally talk about, but I was the one asking questions."

"I think I know something you'd enjoy. Let's go this way." She turned into an alley, and he followed.

"What is it?"

"You'll see."

He wasn't sure he was up for more Briveen surprises. The mandren jerky had worked well, though, so he tried to keep an open mind.

She turned into a doorway with pinwheels above spinning gently in the breeze.

He followed, looking around with interest. He saw nothing particularly remarkable, but Brak must have brought him here for a good reason.

She plucked a metal box off a table and offered it to him. "Ever see one of these?"

He'd seen a great deal over the years. But inside the box was an unfamiliar device. "Some sort of grooming tool?"

"Yes. It's for Briveen youth who still have their biological arms. It's for filing down talons. They tend to get sharp and start catching on everything. Not to mention poking holes."

She flipped the tool open and pantomimed using it.

"Fascinating. So this is a personal care store?"

She set the box back on the table. "In a way. It's a courtesy shop. As you may know, we have a lot of occasions where we give others little token gifts. You can imagine so many compulsory gifts would pile up and become a hassle. To solve that problem, we buy items like these, that we call courtesies. They're useful items that most everyone needs."

"Very sensible."

"We're a sensible people, in general. More than most people realize." She picked up a small item with a handle attached to a flat surface. "This is a scale exfoliator. It's embarrassing to shed a scale in public, so we use this each day to ensure any loose scales are removed." She ran it over her arm, just above her skin, to show how it would be used.

"Also interesting. I've never seen these."

"Of course not. They're too personal to buy from non-Briveen, so we only get them on Briv, and do not ship them as trade goods."

He leaned in close, hoping to avoid being overheard by the store clerk, who stood behind a counter, frowning at an infoboard. "It's okay for me to be here? As an offworlder?"

"Of course. Offworlders have even more occasion to give courtesy gifts. Besides, Prahk there is a friend of mine."

"So he's not refraining from noticing us to avoid a greeting ritual?"

She chuckled. "No. He's just a workaholic. Come meet him."

They approached the sales counter and she said, "Prahk, this is my friend Cabot."

Cabot watched her body language carefully. He saw the posture of a greeting, but only an abbreviated gesture of hello. A very minimal greeting. He followed her lead, reproducing her posture and hand movement.

"I see you've taught him well." Prahk sounded amused, but pleased.

"I haven't taught him much. He knows a great deal about formalities. I thought he'd enjoy seeing a courtesy shop."

Prahk gave a small nod. "Take your time, and let me know if I can help with anything. Any friend of Brak's is a friend of mine. She upgraded my arms, you know. I feel like a teenager." He flexed at the elbows, showing off his cybernetics.

"Wonderful." Cabot meant that sincerely. Sometimes he

forgot that Brak was the premiere cyberneticist in the PAC. Somehow, he'd collected friends in high places.

He liked how welcoming the man seemed. He either didn't notice or didn't care that Cabot was Rescan. It was nice not to immediately be treated like a ripper.

He reached for a bottle of what looked like white lotion. He gave it a sniff. "Hm. No fragrance."

"No." Brak trailed a hand over the counter. "With our sense of smell, adding fragrance is not at all appealing. That's a de-scenting cream, actually. It helps absorb some of our natural body smell. We put it on after a shower."

"So it's like deodorant?"

"Pretty much. But we use it head to toe."

"Wow. I bet this is a popular courtesy gift, then. You must go through a lot of it."

"Yes. It's not hard to make, but it takes time. Easier to buy it if you live on Briv."

He put the cream back. By his estimation, she'd been away from home for fifteen years or more. That meant she'd made a great deal of de-scenting cream for herself. Or maybe she hadn't bothered without other Briveen to worry about. He would not ask her such a personal question.

He was curious about something else, though. "Are you thinking of staying here? There's plenty of work for you on a planet where every adult needs a cybernetics doctor."

She examined another scale exfoliator, a little more closely than it warranted. "I can't say the thought hasn't crossed my mind. But even if my current popularity with the council is more than temporary, I'd face pressure to have children as soon as possible. And I'm not ready to leave the *Onari,* my work, or my friends. Especially not now."

"So you're going back soon?"

"I was planning to get a ride with you, since you'll be

headed right where I need to go. I'd pay for my boarding, of course."

He shook his head. "I'm not a passenger ship."

"So I can't come with you?"

"Of course you can," he answered. "But I don't intend to take your money. I know how underpaid you are, doing pro bono work on the *Onari*."

"I get paid enough. I don't need much."

He tried another strategy. "It's not my ship, my fuel, or my mission. It's Fallon's, and I'm sure she wants you back."

"Very well, then. I accept your terms."

He wondered how Nagali would get along with Brak. Looking at his comport, he reluctantly decided his tour of Briv should come to an end. It was regrettable, but he needed some time to tease out the idea that continued to tickle his nose.

"Time to head back?" Brak asked.

"Yes. I'd love to see more, but I'm here on a job, and I have work to do."

"Of course."

He took care to appreciate everything he saw on the walk back. She'd led them in something of a circle, so the return to the station wasn't long. Again, the pragmatism of the Briveen stood out. They were a practical, intelligent people, and the more he learned about them, the more he liked them.

But how to use all that to figure out how to achieve an accord between them and the PAC?

He'd enjoyed the tour, but was no closer to an answer.

8

ight fell quickly. It seemed that one moment, it was bright and sunny, and the next, Briveen was bathed in moonlight. Cabot's distraction had caused him to miss the transition.

As soon as Brak left after walking him back to his quarters, the others had descended upon him. They'd had no word from the council, and hoped he had. He declined their dinner invitation and closed himself in his quarters again.

He had to figure out this puzzle. He'd hoped the answer would come to him while gazing at Briv, but it hadn't.

His abandoned glass of brandy sat on the table. Sighing, he returned to the chair and swirled the liquid again.

He closed his eyes and let his thoughts wander over the day's events. The realities of Briv versus his expectations. He'd been largely accurate, though there had been surprises. There was nothing like firsthand experience. The museum had been interesting in its choices of subject matter and arrangement. The style of the transit station had begun the spark of an idea that hadn't quite come to fruition.

Brak's ideas about progressiveness, tradition, and necessity made him see her people in a new light. With more sympathy, if he was honest. More understanding. Maybe that was the key element, the thing he hadn't been able to connect. Showing them understanding.

Pragmatism, too. They were a highly sensible people.

Understanding and pragmatism. What else? Those were two points on a line, but he needed a third point to create something bigger, something rounder.

The bolt of realization hit him, straight down the back of his neck, through his spine, and into his stomach.

Survival. Family was key.

The PAC's offer to the Briv needed to be more than protection of their species right now. The PAC needed to ensure their long-term survival. To assist the Briveen in solving their reproductive issues, so they could evolve as a society, rather than cling to ways that people observed when they must but ignored any other time.

The solution would be pragmatic, and Cabot could sell it as such. Yes. He could. He'd sell it in a way that the Briveen could wholeheartedly agree with.

He downed the brandy and smiled.

AT NOON THE NEXT DAY, Cabot felt more alive than he ever had. He was about to put together the biggest deal of his entire career.

He had to play it cool, though.

His group of four made their way to the somber room reserved for diplomacy. Wearing their cloaks, they carefully observed the Briveen customs.

The rituals were long. He hoped Nagali, Omar, and Arlen felt somewhat mollified by the necessity. They'd seemed peeved earlier when they hadn't needed the skills they'd worked so hard to learn. They would all use them to great advantage in the future—few traders had the necessary knowledge to deal with the Briveen, which made the skill highly valuable.

He'd contacted Fallon the night before and gotten a response that morning. Everything was in place. He just had to make the sale.

Rule of Sales Number Twelve: Never let an opportunity slip away.

Gretch made the introductions, and Cabot greeted each of the eight council members, with particular respect paid to the two proconsuls.

Showtime.

As the speaker, Cabot stood while the others sat. It provided him with a stage, and he, undoubtedly, was a performer. He dug deep to deliver the best performance of his life.

"Honorable representatives of the Briveen, now that all the rituals have been performed, I would like to express to you my sincere admiration. Not as a polite necessity, but in genuine wonder at the beauty I've found here." He paced as he spoke, behind his colleagues, who sat at one long table. Across the room, the Briveen faced them from behind an identical table. Then he walked into the space between them. He was truly center stage now.

"I have been in awe of the natural beauty of your planet, and the beauty you've created in your art, architecture and even your culture. You've overcome difficulties through strength and hard choices, but instead of a police state, you've created a place where people have so much respect for one another that they express it every day, every time they come face to face. It is truly an amazing achievement, like none I've ever seen."

He let a silence fall over the room, so his point would carry, and so the Briveen could sense his deep sincerity. He meant every word he said. He'd realized the true beauty of what the

Briveen had accomplished. They'd faced extinction, been forced to implement rules to ensure survival, yet the planet hadn't become some dystopian nightmare. Despite the tedium of the rituals, it was the most peaceful place Cabot had ever seen.

It was time to close the deal.

"In this short time I've been on Briv, I have come to love it. Last night, I communicated with PAC command, explaining what I've realized."

He glanced around at the rapt faces. He had the complete attention of every person in the room. Good. Now, to reveal his pièce de resistance.

He wished he could stretch the moment. There was a special kind of joy in delivering the right thing, at the right time, with just the right flair. Such a thing did not come along often.

"The PAC has launched a large, intensive study on ensuring healthy Briveen genetics. Right now, the funding and the team are being created. The best reproductive specialists in the PAC will participate, and the research will not stop until a solution has been found to increase fertility rates until they are equal to those on Earth."

He let that announcement sit for a moment before continuing, "This initiative will happen regardless of your decision here today. It will happen because it needs to, and it is long overdue. The PAC expresses its sorrow that it has taken this long to attend to this critical need."

He bowed deeply and returned to his chair.

One of the proconsuls—the one named Gerrek—spoke. He had mottled green scales and kind eyes. "We are deeply gratified by what you've said. Our biological limitations have shaped us in more ways than one," he made a small gesture to indicate his arms, "and if the solution to our reproductive difficulties were found, it would open up many opportunities."

The other proconsul, Bret, nodded. "It would be a tremendous gift for our people to have greater choice in our personal lives." She turned her head to look where Brak sat next to Gretch. "And to stop forcing some of our brightest minds to leave."

Brak looked shocked, but Bret shifted her attention to Cabot. "It is my understanding that the PAC wishes to provide us with protection from the Barony Coalition's aggressive incursions on our space. Is that correct, Mr. Layne?"

"Yes," he said simply. "It is."

Gerrek spoke again. "And in return, we would support the PAC by giving them the full output of our manufacturing industry, to be paid for at market value?"

"Yes," Cabot said again.

The proconsuls exchanged a look.

Bret looked to each side of her to include the rest of the council, all of whom had remained silent throughout the proceeding. "It is the opinion of my co-proconsul and I that this is not only an agreeable pact, but a necessary one. By strengthening the PAC, we strengthen ourselves. Even more so now, with their pledge for medical research."

Gerrek added, "It will not be easy to cancel or postpone our existing contracts, but we believe that not doing so would be harder in the long run. This is not a perfect solution, but it is the best we can manage in trying times. Does the council agree?"

When there was silence, Bret asked. "Are there any dissenters?"

More silence.

Hopefully that was a good sign.

Gerrek said, "Normally, we would take at least a day to affirm an agreement of such magnitude. But before coming in here, Bret and I were informed that one of our warships have spotted at least three Barony ships on long-range sensors. Time is of the essence. We may already be too late."

Bret straightened and lifted her chin. "We, the government of Briv, do solemnly bind ourselves to this pact. We accept responsibility for whatever outcomes it may bring." She let out a breath. "In light of the circumstances, we will suspend all due ceremony. Expediency in finalizing this pact is more important."

Cabot was impressed. Brak was right that this group was more progressive than they seemed. He was worried, too, that the situation had become so serious.

"Then I suggest we contact Fallon at Dragonfire Station, and inform her immediately."

Gerrek spread his hands. "I've just sent confirmation, along with my official credentials to verify. Now we can only wait."

TIME PASSED SLOWLY when billions of lives hung in the balance. At least, it did when all Cabot could do was sit and wait.

He wasn't used to being in such a helpless position. Or such an inactive one. He'd done everything he could, rocketing across star systems to get here, open negotiations, and present the deal. Now he was locked out of the action, relegated to sitting and waiting.

A man could fit a lot of thought into a mere few minutes. First, Cabot thought about the luxury he's enjoyed, having felt relatively safe all his life. Sure, he'd flouted many a PAC law in his lifetime, but he'd known he could always flee to a place where those same laws would be enforced to protect him. He'd had access to as much safety as he'd wanted. That might all be obliterated if this deal didn't go through. Not that he thought it likely for the PAC to reject the deal it had initiated, but Cabot had nothing to do but think about eventualities.

He thought about what it would be like to have to evacuate Dragonfire. To lose his home and the community he'd become a part of. Where would he go? Would there be anywhere he *could* go?

Finally, he considered how little he mattered. He'd spent his life receding into the shadows, deriving his satisfaction from seeing to the needs and desires of others. If this was the end of the PAC, and the end of him, had his life been a worthwhile one?

Thirty minutes of introspection later, Fallon's face appeared on the oversized voicecom panel displayed at the head of the room.

"Proconsuls. Council." She bowed her head politely. " We have reviewed your terms, and I'm pleased to see we have an agreement. It is our honor to work with you in this matter."

Bret and Gerrek bowed their heads as well.

Bret said, "Commander, as we've indicated, we have suspended ceremonies in the interest of haste. There are Barony ships headed our way right now, and we do not know their intentions. We doubt they mean anything good for our planet."

"We've been tracking those ships, Proconsul, since they left their own space. And we've dispatched several of our own ships to aid you. The good news is that you will not have to wait weeks for us to arrive. The bad news is that current estimates indicate that, if those Barony ships continue all the way to Briv, they will do so at least twelve hours before our closest ships arrive."

The proconsuls exchanged a long look. "Let's hope their vector carries them past Briv on a routine trade delivery to another system. But I'm glad to know that if they don't, we'll have support."

"You'll have everything we can give you," Fallon promised.

"May I suggest we speak every three hours as the situation develops?"

"We'd welcome that," Gerrek said. "In the meantime, we will begin preparing for what happens if those ships are locked onto our coordinates."

"We'll be doing the same," Fallon affirmed.

"In three hours, then."

The screen went black. Cabot's mood had gone from jubilant to deeply worried.

"How far out are those Barony ships?" Gretch asked. "Assuming they're on a direct course and maintain their current speed."

"They're moving fast, relatively speaking. If they're coming here, we have thirty-six hours to prepare." Bret looked grim.

Cabot hadn't expected this turn of events. Maybe nothing would happen. The Barony vessels might go right by on their way to the Orestes cluster or something. Or they might just be experimenting with how far they could push the PAC.

Or in thirty-six hours, the Briveen could be facing an invasion.

Bret and Gerrek stood.

"We must begin preparing for the worst," Bret said. "I urge all of you, including Brak, to gather your belongings and immediately go to the orbital elevator. You've done your job here, and done it well, but it's in your best interest to get away from here."

Cabot stood, as well. "Is there anything we can do to help?"

Gerrek shook his head. "We'll have all available ships in orbit, and our ground forces will be mobilized. We will also recommend that any offworlders or citizens with ships at the docking station depart within the next four hours, burning hard to get out of range. There's nothing more for you to do here."

"Telling people to leave won't cause a panic?" Nagali asked.

Cabot flinched, hoping the outspokenness of one of his

attendants didn't offend. But the Briveen did not seem bothered.

"We are Briveen," Bret answered. "We will stand with honor."

They would, too, Cabot was certain. They were a magnificent people, in ways he was only just discovering. If he had anything to offer them, he'd remain, but he was no fighter. No pilot. He was just a trader, and a sellout of one, at that.

"May the ancestors watch over you," he said with a low bow of respect.

"And you." Bret said, returning their bow. "Now go, friends. Waste no time."

CABOT HAD IMAGINED the end of this mission many different ways, but none had involved him hurrying back to the *Outlaw* to escape what might, or might not, be a full-scale invasion.

He took no comfort from knowing he would escape. He was glad his companions would be safe. But for once in his life, he wished he were more like Fallon, or one of her team. Someone who fought, and bled, and defended.

Brak escorted them through a labyrinth of corridors to their quarters. Outside Cabot's door, she bowed. "Thank you for your work here. But I will not be leaving with you. If the Barony Coalition does come, my people will fight, and they will need doctors. Please get to the docking station as soon as possible, and get away from here."

He'd known she would stay. In her own way, she had as much of a hero complex as anyone else he knew. "Take care, Brak."

"You too."

Then she was gone.

In his quarters, he threw together his belongings. While

Omar finished his own packing, Cabot carried his luggage next door to the women's quarters. He was sure Arlen would pack quickly, but Nagali might need some prodding.

Upon entering, he was surprised to see her ready to go, sitting on the couch next to her luggage.

She looked up at him. "This makes me sad."

"Because you were hoping to stay here for a while and work some business?"

"No." She frowned. "Well, yes, but that's not what I meant. This just feels so surreal. It's like, what century is this? We're supposed to live in a time when planets don't attack other planets. We don't all have to love each other, but interplanetary war?" Her shoulders sagged.

"The PAC only continues if people support it," he said, setting his bag on a chair.

"I didn't mean the PAC. They don't have a monopoly on peace. And it's never been perfect. I mean just plain being civilized enough to realize that this kind of struggle serves no one."

"And who, besides the PAC, encourages being civilized and peaceful, however imperfectly they might do it?"

She sighed. "Fine. So I'm terrible for operating outside of PAC laws, but wanting them to keep the galaxy in line. I'm a hypocrite."

"Yes, you are, but since you've never started any wars, I'm fine with that."

She fixed him with a stare. "What's your point?"

"I don't have one. I just like arguing with you. Apologies."

She let out a chuckle. "Ridiculous. We're both ridiculous."

"What's ridiculous?" Arlen stepped out of her bedroom carrying her luggage. Cabot wondered what had taken her so long.

"Nothing," Cabot said. "Ready?"

The doors opened and Omar appeared before she could answer. He took a quick look around. "All right. Let's go."

They all exchanged glances, then started for the doors. It wasn't how they expected to end this trip, but there was nothing left for them to do here.

THEY HAD to wait only a few minutes for the orbital elevator to arrive. No one got off.

Cabot felt both relieved and disappointed to board the elevator, stow his luggage, and take a seat. He no longer wore a cloak, and was set to go back to his life as a plain old trader.

He should have felt elated for having done the job he'd been sent to do, but the uncertainty facing Briv overshadowed everything. It wasn't just Briv, either. It was also what Briv's invasion would mean for the PAC. Control of Briv would tip the scales in Barony's favor, enable them to gain more allies.

Only ten people had entered, but the doors closed.

The voicecom announced, "All systems go for ascension."

The elevator began its climb.

Normally, people would chatter during a ride up or down. Cabot's group of four remained silent, and the other six passengers, all non-Briveen, said little amongst themselves.

A loud bang and violent lurch caused screams of fright from the other passengers. A Sarkavian woman had been thrown from her seat, but the human with her helped her up.

"Is she okay?" Omar turned to ask.

The elevator dropped briefly, then came to another hard stop. Cabot felt like he'd he'd been thrown against a wall.

"What's happening?" Nagali asked him, anxious but not panicked.

Cabot could say a lot of things about her, but she had grit.

The voicecom came to life. The person speaking sounded in control, though far less nonchalant than they had previously. "Attention passengers. There has been an equipment failure.

For your safety, you will be returned to the ground via a backup tether. Do not be alarmed. You are only twenty meters up, and will reach the ground in moments."

They began a slow, crawling descent. But they touched down safely and the doors of the elevator reopened.

"Should we get off?" the Sarkavian woman wondered aloud.

The voicecom spoke again. "Passengers, we apologize for the difficulty. Please disembark from the elevator. We will perform maintenance and have it working as soon as possible. Since this may take some time, we suggest you return to your accommodations."

"What about the other elevator?" A man asked, but the voicecom didn't answer.

"Should we go back to our quarters?" Arlen wondered.

"Yes, I think so," Cabot said. "Maybe we can find out what's going on."

Omar grimaced. "I think we already know."

Cabot sighed. "I'm hoping we're wrong."

They weren't wrong.

"Where did the ship come from?" Cabot asked Proconsul Gerrek via the voicecom in Cabot's quarters. Omar sat beside him, while Nagali and Arlen were across the room.

"We believe it was hiding behind one of the moons of an uninhabited planet. It's small, and we didn't see it until it was too late."

"Why would they disable the elevators? That will make it harder for them to get planetside."

The proconsul dipped his head in agreement. "We can only surmise it somehow fits their strategy. Unfortunately, this confirms that those ships are coming here and planning to invade."

"Have you talked to Fallon?"

"Bret is speaking with Jamestown now. Fallon will be informed by the regular PAC chain of command."

"Right. Of course." Cabot felt foolish. Fallon might be his contact in the PAC command, but she would not be in charge of an event like this.

"I'm sorry you're now stuck here with the rest of us, but glad you weren't hurt. Please remain in your quarters. The station is heavily fortified, and will be well-protected. It's the safest place you could be right now." Gerrek looked regretful.

"We'll be fine," Cabot assured him. "Thank you for calling on us. We won't keep you further—I'm sure you're overburdened as it is."

"Yes. There is much to do."

The screen went black, leaving Cabot and Omar looking at each other in silence.

Omar spoke first. "So we just sit here, waiting for the invasion?"

"That's what he said."

Omar's right eyelid lowered, a sure sign that he intended to disobey. "Yeah, I don't think so. If we're stuck here, let's find a way we can help."

Cabot smiled. "I was thinking the same thing. I'll see if I can get hold of Brak. Since she didn't do as she was told either, she might have some ideas of how we can be useful."

J‍UDGING from Brak's face and posture via the voicecom display, she was not delighted to hear from him. "You should remain at the station. Soon, they will be evacuating the upper levels to the underground shelter. Citizens will be directed there, as well as other designated disaster shelters."

Alarm zinged up Cabot's spine. That seemed like an

extreme move at this point. "Why?"

Brak clacked her teeth. "According to Gretch, Barony ships launched missiles in advance of their arrival. Most likely, they intend to create maximum chaos to distract and weaken us before their ships arrive."

"Will defensive systems be able to destroy the missiles?"

"Unknown. It's possible."

He recognized prevarication when he saw it. "But not likely."

"No. The latest in missile technology makes them able to spoof their coordinates, making it difficult to get a positive lock until it's too late."

He let out a slow breath. "So, what's the plan?"

"There are few options. Normally, small, fast ships would be deployed from the docking station. We have no access to those ships, since the station was damaged along with the elevators, leaving us unable to release those vessels. We can only send up ships capable of atmospheric landings, and there are few small, fast ships that can do that."

A piece of knowledge clicked into place in his mind. "Gretch has one. I've obtained parts for it. He's going up, isn't he?"

"Yes. He's a greatly skilled pilot, and he knows his ship better than anyone. Hopefully he can detonate those missiles while they're far enough from Briv that they won't matter."

As a connoisseur of people, Cabot could divine the other thing she wasn't telling him. "You're going with him."

She dipped her head in acknowledgement. "The military we have on the ground is preparing for battle or beginning evacuations. With my background in science, I am as qualified to assist him as just about anyone else, aside from a weapons specialist."

He had a feeling he would regret his next words. "Then I suggest you take me with you as well. I'm a specialist of many things that are bought and sold, including weapon systems for ships. I'm particularly familiar with the capabilities of Gretch's ship, since I sold that weapon system to him, along with various propulsion upgrades."

She silently watched him through the display for a long moment. "You have technological expertise about these systems?"

"Yes. I'm no mechanic, but I know the components I sell inside and out."

Brak let out a heavy breath. "Then you should come with us."

"Don't act so happy about it." He probably shouldn't make jokes, but he knew from long experience that humor could act as a lifeline in a crisis.

"I'm glad for the assistance. Gretch will be, as well. I'm just sorry it's going to put you in harm's way."

"We're all in harm's way. I might as well be doing something to help rather than cowering in a shelter."

Amusement lightened the seriousness in her eyes. "That's something we have in common." She rolled her shoulders back. "Right, then. I'll be by the station shortly, and we'll proceed together to Gretch's launchpad."

"He has his own launchpad? He'd been holding out on me. Once all this is over, I'm going to give him an additional ten percent markup."

Brak let out a snort of laughter. "I'll see you in about fifteen minutes. Meet me on the north side of the station, outside the side entrance."

"Is it safe out there?"

Her chin lifted with pride. "Yes. And it will remain so for as long as we keep Barony away. My people will not go crazy when they realize what's happening. There will be no looting, no trampling one another. A time of crisis is an opportunity to show our true honor."

Impressive. "Fifteen minutes, then."

Having a plan of action, however crazy and dangerous it seemed, felt better than being helpless.

"Then I'm going with you," Nagali declared.

Cabot suppressed a groan. If there was a time he did not need Nagali throwing herself into something, it was now.

"Absolutely not. I'm going because I can serve a purpose. There's no reason for you to go."

"Yes. There is." She sighed, produced a tiny knife from her voluminous right sleeve, then pulled back her left sleeve to expose her arm to her shoulder.

Omar let out a yelp of surprise when Nagali cut into the flesh of her underarm. "Be a dear and get me a towel, Omar."

Muttering, he did as he was told.

Arlen exchanged a wide-eyed look of disbelief with Cabot, but he was far less shocked than he probably should be. It was Nagali, after all. She could do little to surprise him. He felt grimly confident that whatever she was about to reveal would be terrible.

And it was.

She pinched something black and about the size of a small marble from the inside of her upper arm. After using the towel to blot her arm and then the item, she held it in her palm for them to see.

"What is it?" Arlen asked.

Nagali looked entirely too pleased with herself. "Look."

She opened the black sphere and let a tiny green ball roll into her palm.

"Prelin's ass," Omar breathed. His shocked gaze went to Cabot. "I swear I didn't know about this."

Cabot knew Brivinium when he saw it. He'd been unfortunate enough to have a large quantity of it on his hands not that long ago. Since Arlen had been the one to unintentionally bring it to him, she also recognized it on sight.

"You had that with you all this time? Under your skin? You could have blown us all up at any moment!" Arlen's eyes had opened even wider.

Nagali scoffed. "It's in a priyanomine case, lined with an inert layer, to prevent sensors from detecting it. It would have combusted only if we were in an explosion or thrown into an acid bath. Both cases seemed unlikely, and I figured, if either of those things happened, we wouldn't much care if this thing blew up."

Omar groaned and put his hands to his face.

Cabot refused to let her see him ruffled. "What was your plan for that?" He pointed to the sphere in her palm.

"I found it in a rock collection, if you can believe that. The Brivinium had been stolen, no doubt, and cut down to lessen its danger and make it easier to smuggle. Someone must have acquired it and figured it to be some semi-precious rock. I had only come across it just before you came to Dauntless. When I found out where you were headed, and I didn't even have to con you to get a ride, I figured it was fate."

Oh, he hated her blasé dismissal of a highly volatile, highly illegal-anywhere-but-on-Briv substance. Still, he had to admire her cleverness and willingness to take a risk.

He sighed. "We will discuss the events that led up to now after we manage to survive our current situation. I'll take the Brivinium and give it to Gretch. He can decide what to do with it."

"Absolutely not!" Nagali's fist closed around the sphere. "Either I'll hand it to him, or you'll have to cut off my hand."

Omar rolled his eyes. "Let's not be melodramatic." He looked to Cabot. "But if she's going, I'm going."

Arlen spoke up. "I'm not staying behind. I'm a good pilot, and can assist Gretch."

Cabot sighed. He had only five minutes to get outside and meet Brak. No time to argue.

"Fine. Let's go."

"I AGREED to let *you* come, not everyone you know on this planet." Brak was not as displeased as she could have been, under the circumstances, but she was less than delighted.

"Unfortunately, we're a package deal." Cabot lifted his shoulder and ducked his head in a Briveen expression of apology.

"We don't have time to argue. Let's go." She led them to a groundcar, a boxy, utilitarian vehicle that, fortunately, was made for large people.

They all just barely fit, with Nagali sitting on Omar's lap. Omar had suggested Arlen, but she had enthusiastically declined.

Cabot was too preoccupied to enjoy his first car ride on Briv, or appreciate the lovely views that blurred by his window.

No one was inclined to talk. Not even Nagali. She appeared to be distracted by the scenery. Her arm might be sore where she'd cut it. They'd only had time to bandage. Or maybe she was thinking about the Brivinium she'd tucked into a pouch under her clothes.

He tried not to imagine what the car would look like if it exploded, and how far the shrapnel would travel.

He didn't know Briveen road laws, but he was sure, by the way they all leaned sideways during turns, Brak was traveling faster than normal.

The urban landscape shifted, becoming less closely packed. They transitioned into rural surroundings, which made sense.

A ship couldn't take off from the surface in the middle of a city. The thrust necessary required a good deal of explosive force.

Outside the city, Brak drove even faster. Cabot wondered if they'd make it to Gretch's launchpad in one piece.

An hour later, they came to a quick stop behind a retaining wall.

"Let's go!" Brak barked, and they evacuated the car, hustling to the outbuilding.

A guard waited inside. He said something in Brivinian, the words sounding low and growly to Cabot, and Brak ushered them out again.

"They're near the end of the launch sequence. If we were ten minutes later, he'd have left without us."

Cabot wasn't accustomed to running. He preferred a sedate stroll and struggled to keep up with Brak.

Arlen had her arm around Nagali's waist to hasten her on. It was a brave thing to do, considering what Nagali carried under her clothes.

The hatch was open, its stairs folded down, and they ran into the ship, each one of them on the heels of the person before.

"Go!" Brak shouted to the pilot.

Behind them, the hatch hissed as it closed, folding upward and inward.

"You'd better strap in!" Gretch's voice shouted over the noise that had suddenly amped up a couple hundred decibels.

Brak led them up to the cockpit, which was about the size of the *Outlaw's*. Arlen took the copilot seat and Cabot sat at the science station. Brak occupied weapons control, and Omar folded down a jump seat and put his straps on.

"Headsets are under your seats!" Gretch yelled.

Cabot settled them over his ears, and the noise mercifully retreated. The others did the same.

Gretch's voice came over a channel in the headsets. "I don't know why there are so many of you, but you're stuck now. Double-check your straps. If you've never done an atmospheric launch, this is going to be quite an experience."

Brivinian words came over the headset and Gretch spoke back to the control station. Then the countdown began.

Ten…nine…eight…

When they got to *one*, the ship shuddered. The Briveen guard barked something that was undoubtedly, "Ignition" or "Launch!"

Even with the inertial dampeners, tremendous pressure forced Cabot into his seat, making it impossible to move. Making it hard to breathe.

"Hang in there," Gretch said over the headset, though his voice was thin and strained.

Two minutes felt like an eternity when every breath was a struggle and Cabot felt like he'd be crushed any second. But then they cleared Briv's exosphere and the atmospheric drag let go of them.

Cabot was never so glad to breathe freely.

"Everyone okay?" Gretch asked.

They all made some sort of affirmative sound.

"Good. The coordinates of the missiles are already locked in, and we will intercept them in forty minutes. We can remove our headsets now."

After they'd all done so, Nagali turned her head to look at Cabot. He nodded.

She said, "I have something. I don't know if it helps."

Brak and Gretch twisted around to look back at her.

"What?" Brak asked.

Nagali struggled to get beneath her straps and then under her shirt to reach the pouch. After a third failed attempt, she burst out, "Ugh! Can I take off the straps?"

Gretch nodded, and Nagali freed herself, removed the pouch, and handed it to Brak.

Brak cupped one palm and tipped the contents of the pouch out into it. The tiny green orb rolled out. Brak stared. Gretch stared. Then they both stared at Nagali.

"I didn't steal it," she said defensively. "It was in a rock collection someone was selling. They didn't know. I was just bringing it back where it belonged."

"To sell?" Gretch asked, eyeing her dubiously.

"No! To give back the Briveen's rightful property."

"For free?" Brak also looked doubtful.

Nagali sighed. "Yes. For free. I was hoping it would open some doors for me to develop some trade ties here." Then she added, "But I did want to see it get home."

Brak tiled her hand, making the sphere roll. "I've never even seen it in person."

Gretch took off his straps and leaned close. "Neither have I."

Cabot found that surprising. Two Briveen natives who had never seen Brivinium and he'd seen it twice. He really did lead an eventful life.

"What do we do with it?" Arlen asked.

That got the Briveens' attention. They looked at each other, wearing calculating expressions.

"It won't help with the missiles. All we need to do is destroy their guidance systems. Either they go out into space to blow up, or we force them to explode right away. Either way, they won't enter Briv's atmosphere."

"You make it sound easy," Omar noted.

"It isn't." Gretch's voice was flat. "There are three missiles, and we have to be directly between them and Briv. Then we'll need to target their guidance systems, while they're moving, without knocking them right into Briv. It doesn't take much firepower, but it takes tremendous precision."

"So the Brivinium's useless?"

Again, he and Brak exchanged a look. She nodded.

"Not useless," Gretch said. "It's not helpful with the

missiles, but it would be just about right for a Barony warship."

Gretch and Brak watched them for reactions.

Arlen nodded. "Let's do it."

"I'm in," Omar added.

"I'd be disappointed if we didn't use the Brivinium," Nagali said.

They were all crazy. And so was he. Cabot said, "We're all in. Let's take down a warship."

THEY DIDN'T TALK as they counted down the minutes. They had gone over the plan so they were ready to act, but they waited it out in silence.

Finally, Gretch said, "There." His eyes were locked on the display. "Arrival in two minutes. All hands, prepare for action."

Gretch and Brak had done all the math. They'd calculated the vectors, the angles, and the timing, down to the second. Seconds meant the difference between success and letting those missiles land on Briv.

Gretch maintained the proper position, and they all held their breath as the missiles approached. "We're on target," he said tersely.

"Brak, get ready. Fire in five...four...three...two...one. Fire!" Then he said, "Second target in three...two...one...fire! And third target. Two...one...fire!"

From his seat in the back, Cabot couldn't see the display, but he heard a sigh from Brak and Gretch.

"Two targets destroyed," Brak said. "One target is spinning toward uninhabited space."

Gretch allowed himself a mere moment to relish their success. Then he twisted around to look at them again. "Time to intercept the first warship is five hours if we burn hard. Seven if we leave enough left to get us back to Briv."

"Let's err on the side of having a chance to survive," Cabot suggested.

He was surrounded by murmurs of agreement.

"Glad we're all on the same page," Gretch said. "Intercept in seven hours, then. Coordinates and speed locked in. Now we wait. Again."

YOU CAN SAY the word *warship*. You can imagine its purpose. But there's nothing like watching hundreds of thousands of metric tons of metal bear down on you while you sit in a teeny little ship.

Cabot felt like he'd slipped into a parallel universe. This wasn't his life. He was supposed to be on Dragonfire, selling things to people.

But here he was, trying to save a planet with his ex-wife, ex-brother-in-law, and some friends.

"We have two options," Gretch said. "We can load the brivinium onto a torpedo. It's simple, and all we have to do is make sure the torpedo hits its target. However, we run the risk of the launch setting off the brivinium."

"In which case the only thing getting blown up would be us," Brak added, quite unnecessarily.

"Second option?" Omar asked, sounding peeved.

"We drop the sphere in their path, wait for them to come into range, then hit them with a torpedo. That's less of an immediate risk to us, but instead of aiming at just one thing, we have to juggle three variables."

"Probabilities of success of each?" Nagali asked, her tone so dry it was almost sarcastic.

Cabot sent her a warning glance.

Brak spoke. "Option one, thirty percent chance of success, give or take ten percent. Also, a twenty-four percent chance of our own destruction."

"Those are bad odds," Omar observed.

Brak ignored him. "Option two, twenty percent chance of success, give or take twenty percent, and a five percent chance of our own destruction."

"That's not very helpful," Arlen said. She didn't sound irritated, just perplexed.

"I vote for option two," Cabot said. "It's more complicated, but I think it's more likely to succeed."

"I kind of want to see if we'd blow ourselves up, but I agree option two sounds better," Nagali said.

They all took a moment to stare at her.

"There's something wrong with you," Omar told her. "Always has been." He shook his head. "But I vote option two as well."

The others nodded.

"Looks like we're unanimous," Gretch said. "Okay. Let's get on the calculations. First, we have to know where to drop the brivinium. That will determine what position we need to hold, and when we must fire. We'll want to calculate multiple scenarios, and have formulas in place so we can make adjustments if necessary."

For two hours, he and Brak poked away at the voicecom, crunching numbers, while the rest of them watched their fingernails grow.

"Oh, sure," Omar said. "Just hanging out in space, doing power math so we can save a planet. You know. As one does."

Arlen and Nagali laughed, and even Cabot had to smile.

"It's not like the holo-vids, is it?" he asked.

"Nothing ever is," Arlen agreed. She shifted her attention to Nagali. "Well, except maybe for you."

They laughed again, earning themselves a dirty look from Brak, who was trying to concentrate.

"Sorry," Cabot said.

An hour later, math had given them a plan. They had coordinates, timing, trajectories and kilometers of calculations.

"And the scientists shall inherit the planet," Omar intoned dramatically, resulting in snickers.

Gretch murmured to Brak, "What are they talking about?"

Brak answered quietly, "I don't know. Sometimes simian humor still eludes me."

The rest of them laughed.

"Okay," Gretch announced. "We're at the coordinates. Nagali, since you brought this thing, I think you should be the one to drop it out the airlock."

Nagali rose. "It will be my honor. I'll try not to drop it too soon."

She held it at chin level, cupped in both hands, like a priestess with an offering, and disappeared down the corridor.

"I can't believe you trusted her with it," Omar cracked. "We're all dead for sure."

That time, they all laughed.

THE TINY BRIVINIUM sphere hovered in space like a speck of dust. It was nothing. Invisible. If they hadn't tagged it, they wouldn't even know it was there.

They worried the warship might deviate from its course, but it apparently thought them too insignificant to bother with. As it probably should. But it didn't know what they knew. So on it came.

While they waited, they exchanged more inappropriate humor, with Brak and Gretch gamely trying to play along. What else could they do? If it all went wrong, at least they'd passed their last hours in camaraderie and humor. A person could do worse.

9

The voicecom came to life, startling them all. "Briveen vessel, this is the *P.A.C.S. Roosevelt*. Please break off your maneuvers and get as far from here as you can."

Cabot and Arlen stared at each other. Then he looked at the others, who were equally stunned.

"They're early," Omar said.

"How did we not detect their approach?" Gretch wondered, poking commands into the voicecom. "I still don't read them. I've got nothing on sensors."

"They have some sort of sensor-blocking technology on their ship." Brak sounded as amazed as the rest of them.

"I think we should answer them," Cabot said.

Gretch hit the communications circuit. "*Roosevelt,* this is the Briveen airship *Talon*. Advising you that we have just lined that ship's path with a ball of Brivinium. Transmitting the coordinates and withdrawing from the area."

"That's it?" Arlen complained. "All that buildup, and we just mosey away?"

"Nope," Gretch said. "We're going to get to a safe distance

and watch. Hang on." After a few minutes, he said, "Here. Just in time."

He brought up the image of the Barony ship, still on course for the Brivinium. Finally, they were in range.

Cabot held his breath.

A minute passed.

Then the *Roosevelt* fired, not at the Barony ship, but at the Brivinium.

The directed burst created a traveling cone of explosion, enveloping the ship and continuing to explode out and away from the *Roosevelt*.

Cabot had never seen anything like it. Explosions out in space were never the big fiery balls of flame and fire that happened within an atmosphere, but tended to be a brief light and then an implosion, and blackness. But this was electrical. Cabot could see the energy readings, which registered higher than anything he'd ever seen.

The Barony burned itself out and turned black in seconds, imploding into a husk.

It gave Cabot no satisfaction, except the relief of knowing it would not come after Briv.

Now that the PAC was there to ensure the planet's safety, all was as it should be.

Like it needed to continue to be, for all the allied planets.

Cabot felt something in him shift, like a telescope changing its focus from something close to something much further away. If this thing with Barony was going to continue, he needed to help fight them in his own way.

They could have lost Briv that day. It could have been the day that went down in infamy as the turn of the Barony War, as, perhaps, it would come to be known. But it wasn't. Today wasn't the day, and he wanted to do whatever he could to make sure tomorrow wouldn't be, either. Or the day after.

He wasn't a soldier. He wasn't a diplomat. But he could help. He would.

He had a sudden, strange moment of understanding for his friends with hero complexes. Cabot Layne was no hero. But he had a nose, and friends to look after.

It wasn't the same thing, but it was enough.

CABOT HAD NEVER BEEN SO glad to return to Dragonfire. He stepped out of the airlock onto the boardwalk, *his* boardwalk, and stood for a long minute. He closed his eyes and drank in the sounds and smells of home. Most people here did not yet know about the battle the PAC had waged at Briv, and the tragedy it had averted.

He envied their innocence. They didn't know how hard life might get. The possibilities didn't even exist to them yet. If he'd felt protective of his community here before, he felt so much more so now.

He wondered if that was how Fallon felt, with all she did and all she knew. He'd never want her job, that was for sure, but he wanted to help protect the people here in his own way.

He'd figure out how later.

"You okay?" Arlen stepped out behind him.

"Much better than okay." He opened his eyes, pleased to see people going on about their business as usual.

"Are you sad that Omar and Nagali stayed on Briv?"

"No. They'll be along eventually. Especially when they need something." He chuckled.

Brak stepped out of the docking bay, stopping next to Cabot. She took a deep breath. "Mm, I smell mandren. I'm starved. You two want to join me for lunch?"

"Sure," Cabot agreed.

Arlen nodded. "That sounds great."

A thought occurred to Cabot. "Do you think they have that mandren on a stick?"

Brak nodded. "Definitely."

"I think I'll have one of those along with my Bennite stew."

He smiled as they walked together toward the food shops. His trip to Briv had changed him in more ways than one.

But it was good to be home.

MESSAGE FROM THE AUTHOR

Thank you for reading!

I write because books were always my first love, and I'm thrilled to share these worlds with you. But writing is my job, too, and to make a living from it, I need support from readers like you.

Reviews are critical to my being able to keep bringing you new books, so if you enjoyed this story and can spare a minute or two to leave a review on Amazon, I'd be grateful.

Please sign up for my newsletter at www.ZenDiPietro.com to receive updates on new releases, sales, and other news about my writing.

Are you ready for more Mercenary Warfare? You can read more of Cabot, Omar, and Nagali in *Blood Money*.

In gratitude,
Zen DiPietro

ABOUT THE AUTHOR

Zen DiPietro is a lifelong bookworm, dreamer, and writer. Perhaps most importantly, a Browncoat Trekkie Whovian. Also red-haired, left-handed, and a vegetarian geek. Absolutely terrible at conforming. A recovering gamer, but we won't talk about that. Particular loves include badass heroines, British accents, Kpop music, and the smell of Band-Aids.

Printed in Great Britain
by Amazon